D1706818

RED VELVET VILLAINY

BOOK SEVEN IN THE CUPCAKE CRIMES SERIES

MOLLY MAPLE

MARY E. TWOMEY, LLC

RED VELVET VILLAINY

Book Seven in the Cupcake Crimes Series

By

Molly Maple

COPYRIGHT

Valentine's Day is about to take a turn for the worse.

Charlotte McKay has a passion for baking cupcakes, but when the owner of the Soup Alleyoop restaurant is attacked, she trades in her baking hat for a chef's apron to help in the kitchen making soups. The beloved Gus wouldn't hurt a fly, so when he ends up in the hospital after being attacked, no one quite knows where to point the finger.

With the restaurant hanging on by a thread and a criminal on the loose, Charlotte knows she will have to solve this crime with a soup ladle in one hand and a cupcake pan in the other. When it becomes clear that there is more to the coveted soup recipes than meets the eye, Charlotte is certain that the person who attacked Gus won't stop until the sweet old man is silenced once and for all.

"Red Velvet Villainy" is filled with layered clues and cozy moments, written by Molly Maple, which is a pen name for a USA Today bestselling author.

THE SOUP ALLEYOOP

*I*f an onlooker were to guess at which person would have more pep in their step on a crisp February morning, the safe bet would normally be on the twenty-eight-year-old, rather than the ninety-one-year-old woman. But today, my great-aunt Winifred outpaces me easily as she makes her way from my red sedan into the restaurant.

I'm not totally sure why this particular place stood out to Aunt Winnie as the perfect location for the Valentine's Day party she wants to throw. The Live Forever Club is always up to something fun—casino nights, skinny dipping, painting by moonlight... The three elderly women I adore are the shining stars of the cozy town of Sweetwater Falls. I wouldn't have thought the Soup Alleyoop would be on Aunt Winnie's radar of venues for a

Valentine's Day Roaring Twenties-themed party, but I've learned my aunt is rarely wrong when it comes to showing the world how to have a great time.

I have only been in this restaurant once, being that I am still considered new in town. I have been proud to call Sweetwater Falls my home for over half a year now, but even that amount of time hasn't been enough to draw me back to a restaurant that is part basketball arcade games, part restaurant that only sells soup.

It's a niche market, I can say that.

The faux gymnasium honey-colored wood floors do not announce fine dining, though the place is clean enough. I recall the waitstaff wearing referee outfits with whistles dangling around their necks.

I look around at the red carpeted walls and the sports memorabilia in frames scattered about the place and wonder how much work this venue will take to jazz it up for the Live Forever Club's event.

Aunt Winnie presses the back of her hand to her cheek to warm it from the frigid snowy outdoors. "Yoo-hoo! Gus! Anybody here?" She cranes her neck after stomping the snow off her boots, but there is no one at the counter where you order your food.

I shrug. "Are we early?" I glance to the side to check the large neon scoreboard that tells the time. "Three minutes early. I'm sure they're just in back, firing up the soups. Why don't you walk me around and tell me what you want for your event? I've never been to a Valentine's Day event in Sweetwater Falls." I bat my lashes at her. "Is it all romantic and filled with pink paper hearts?"

Aunt Winnie chortles at my guess that I didn't think would be all that far off the mark. "Romance is for every day, if you want it. Valentine's Day around here is for intrigue. Fun. Mischief. Memories." She bats her hand at me. "Pink paper hearts aren't all that mischievous, so I pass on those."

I press my hand over my sternum and feign a gasp. "Mischief? You? I don't believe it."

Aunt Winnie takes her mittens off and stuffs them in the pockets of her winter coat. She loops her arm through mine and moves me toward the tables. "We want the theme to be the shadier side of the twenties. These booths are perfect. We can convert them into mini speak easies. Imagine everyone all dressed up in their best flapper wear, ordering fancy cocktails and whispering salacious secrets."

I smile at my aunt's vision for the party. "That sounds fun."

"More than fun. Everyone is going to have a mission when they get here. A secret they have to solve."

"For example?"

Aunt Winnie's sea-green eyes dance with mischief. "You'll walk in and be handed a folded piece of paper. Maybe yours will say something like, 'Make sure the bartender puts three olives in your martini.' Then someone else will get a piece of paper that reads, 'Find the person who has three olives in their martini and ask them what sort of socks they think the mayor wears when he goes dancing.' Things like that. Finish your mission and come get another." She elbows me. "I was thinking of having some cute cigarette girls, only instead of handing out cigarettes, they'll hand out the secret missions."

I clap at her playful nature. "Conversation starters that work like a covert game. I love it!"

I know my best friend won't have a single issue with getting all dressed up with fancy twenties-style hairdos so we can play along with the Live Forever Club's hijinks.

I smile at my great-aunt, wondering how I got so lucky that I get to be the one with whom she shares her imagination. "And you think the Soup Alleyoop is the place for your party?"

Aunt Winnie motions around the sports-themed dining area. "I wouldn't mind having it here. It's a nice, open space in the center, which we'll need when the dancing starts. We'll bring in our own hors d'oeuvres and a bartender, so the menu isn't an issue."

Thank goodness. I love soup as much as the next girl, but it's not on my top list of things to eat on Valentine's Day.

Aunt Winifred hums to herself, motioning to the end of the room. "I'm bringing in a swing band. We're going to have a platform built over there, and dancing in the center area here."

Her hips begin to sway. Her eyes close because she is transporting herself either to the distant past or to the near future, where there will be a Valentine's Day party in which there will definitely be dancing.

Aunt Winifred keeps her eyes closed as she turns to me and scoops up my hand in a quickstep. I am uneducated in how to follow with any sort of prowess. Though, I waste no time trying to keep up. I wish I knew how to dance, but with my five-foot-ten inches and zero musical training, I was destined to move like the Tin Man in desperate need of an oil can.

Aunt Winnie doesn't mind my mechanical movements. What she would mind is me not moving at all—not trying to live a little, even if I manage the feat ungracefully.

I trip over my own two feet when she tries to twirl me, which is to be expected. I laugh without holding back, as is my way around any member of the Live Forever Club. "You're about to find out what a dreadful dancer I am."

"Nonsense." Aunt Winnie uses my hand to guide me in and out, her feet shuffling quicker and with more skill than I can muster in my clunky winter boots.

Clumsy as I am, I don't mind the levity one bit. "You need to give me lessons, or I'm going to embarrass myself on the dance floor at the party."

Aunt Winnie hums the melody that we dance to, ending our quickstep when she pulls me in and gives a big "da-da-ta" finish. Then she turns us and bows to our imaginary audience, batting her free hand at them. "Oh, go on.

Stop your wild applause! What, you've never seen two heartbreakers dance the night away?"

I giggle through my bow. "Please tell me the dancing at your party will be just as lively. I've never received an imaginary standing ovation before, if you can believe it."

"I absolutely don't believe it. You're a natural on the dance floor." Aunt Winnie glances around the place to avoid my dubious look at her flagrant compliment. "You could be receiving a real standing ovation if the manager was here." Her smile falls. "Where is Gus?"

The front door opens, triggering the chime overhead, which is a recording of a roaring crowd. As silly as this restaurant is, I like the extra touches that make it truly unique.

I mean, if there were two Soup Alleyoops in the world, that would be an oddity I would need to see to believe.

The person walking into the restaurant is a guy who can't be older than sixteen, which seems to be the key demographic for this place. He carries a basketball under his arm and looks to be ready to put it to use.

He waves to us, nodding to Aunt Winifred. "Hey, Winnie. My mom is real excited for your Valentine's Day thing." He grins, showing off his braces. "My dad is mad at you because he doesn't want to get dressed up. He says people owned sweatpants back in the nineteen-twenties, so he should be able to wear them to the party, no problem." He snorts his amusement as he moseys his lanky form to the empty ordering station. "I think my mom is going to win that argument."

Aunt Winifred strolls over to him, taking me along with her when she loops her arm through mine. "She'd better. I've been known to turn away people who don't take parties seriously."

"Parties are a serious business?" I ask her.

Aunt Winifred nods without caveat. "Absolutely. There is nothing more important than fun." She tilts her head up at the high school student. "Greg, have you met my niece yet?"

"You're the new girl, right? The Cupcake Queen? That's what my little sister calls you."

If there is anything that can pull a grin to my face, it is that label. "Cupcake Queen? That is quite the honor. I'm Charlotte. And yes, I own the Bravery Bakery. Something tells me your little sister might just be one of my favorite people in Sweetwater Falls if that's what she calls me."

"Her birthday is next week, and my mom promised her she was going to place an order of cupcakes for her birthday party. But my sister is waiting for your flavor of the month to come out before she commits to which kinds she wants."

My hand flies to my heart. "What's your sister's favorite flavor?" I decide on the spot that I am going to open up a new facet of my business. "I might just throw in an extra special cupcake for her because it's her birthday."

Birthday cupcakes. That's a thing, right? It takes me a

total of ten seconds to decide that yes, if you place a cupcake order for your birthday, then you get a bonus cupcake, which is a birthday cupcake. I can add a checkbox on the website so they can mark if the order is to celebrate a birthday.

Greg chatters away, grinning while he talks. "It's a big one, too. Double digits. Gracie is turning ten. And she likes anything with sprinkles. The more the better. Like, if you can see the frosting, it's not enough sprinkles."

A thrill lifts my posture so that I am bobbing on my toes. "That's wonderful! I'll make sure she gets her birthday cupcake. Extra sprinkles."

Greg cranes his neck to see if he can peek into the back, where there are smells of soup, but no bustling in the kitchen area to clue us in as to whether or not the staff is actually here. "I was hoping to get in a few rounds of free-throw practice before I have to start my homework, but I don't see anybody." He cups his hands over his mouth. "Hey, Gus! I'm about to start shooting hoops without ordering anything. I think you're going to give me that exasperated smile that means you're secretly frustrated but are too nice to say anything about it." Greg glances around when there is no response.

"Maybe he's not here yet." Aunt Winnie frowns at the empty counter. "But then why was the front door unlocked?"

Greg shrugs and then slaps Aunt Winifred's hand on

his way to the other side of the restaurant, where the free-throw hoop is set up. "I tried."

While I am content to try calling the restaurant to bring someone to the phone, Aunt Winnie has her own way of speeding things up.

She has no qualms going behind the desk where people place their orders, even as I shout-whisper to her that we aren't supposed to be behind the desk, because we are not employees.

Aunt Winnie waves off my worry. "Oh, pish-posh, honey cake. We tried following the rules. Now we're going to see what's cooking back here, so we can get to some serious party planning."

"Isn't that an oxymoron? Serious and parties?"

Aunt Winnie draws her short stature up, tossing her silver curls over her shoulder. "Darling, I am always serious about parties."

I love that she can say things like that with total confidence. Her war cry for me has been that I will become Charlotte the Brave, but it is only in spending time with her that I am learning how to find my voice and really put some volume to it.

I take a deep breath as if preparing to go underwater, then I steal behind the desk that is surely for employees only.

I feel like I am in grade school, doing something I know I should not and hoping the teacher doesn't find out. My stomach knots because I don't want to get in trouble, especially not by this Gus person, whom I don't know. If his first encounter with me is trespassing in his kitchen, I will for sure be a horrible person in his mind.

I hate breaking rules, yet it seems that if I am going to keep up with the Live Forever Club, one day, I'll need to get used to living on the wrong side of the law.

Or the wrong side of the counter, as it were.

As soon as I step where I shouldn't be, a foul smell hits my nose. I pride myself on being able to pick out notes of even the smallest flavor in a recipe, but this stench makes me wish my nose wasn't quite so perceptive.

"Ack. Scorched tomatoes and something rotting. Gross," I mumble to myself. Here's hoping that the menu for the big party smells better than this. If soup is the only thing on their menu, I certainly hope this isn't their prized product, because I cannot imagine anyone ordering seconds.

Aunt Winnie has no such qualms about the smell or her intrusion into the sacred space as she moseys through the narrow kitchen. "Gus? Oh, goodness."

I rush to her side when I see the problem. There is a pot of soup on the stove that has boiled over. My nose crinkles as I cast around for oven mitts. "That's going to be a pain to clean up." The tomato soup has splattered all over the industrial stove, giving the entire area a spattered red paint job.

Aunt Winnie turns off the burner while I locate two oven mitts so I can move the pot off the heat source.

I wince when the soup spits its burning lava onto the tender flesh of my wrist. "Oh! That stings."

Once I have the pot off the burner, I rush to the sink and run my wrist under a stream of icy water. I hiss through gritted teeth when the burn doesn't cool quick enough for my liking. While I've burned myself loads of times, the inside of my wrist has never toughened up.

Aunt Winnie winces. "Oo, that's going to leave a mark."

After I turn off the water, I cast around for something with which to dry off. My feet take me to the closet next to the back exit to search for a towel, and to clean up the tomato splatters on the surfaces and floor.

Aunt Winnie clucks her tongue, and I know she is thinking she can't believe the kitchen was left with a burner on. Aside from the food being ruined, it's a safety hazard I am grateful we were here to fix. "This isn't like Gus. He would never leave his kitchen messy. He's an orderly sort of man. Keeps a clean house. The business is always spotless." She frowns, looking around at the state of the stove and floor. "I don't understand."

I wipe down my kitchen every time I use it. Being without a space to create my own cupcake flavors for so long has made me extra appreciative of the industrial kitchen I now have.

But when I open the closet door, the mess of the kitchen is the last thing on my mind.

"Ah!" I shout incoherently. I don't mean to startle Aunt

Winnie, but I am not sure there is an elegant or tranquil response to announce what I am seeing.

Horror twists my pleasant expression as I take in the man on the floor, who is bound, gagged and limp against the mop and bucket. His legs are bent at uncomfortable angles, suggesting he was shoved into the closet after he was attacked.

Aunt Winnie is at my side, her mouth agape. "It's Gus! Quick, Charlotte, call Logan. Call a doctor, too!" She leans in as I take a step back. "Gus! Oh, dear. Is he..." Her voice catches at the possibility that her friend might be here only in body but not in spirit.

I fumble with my phone and place the quickest call I can manage because polite language escapes me. "Gus... Soup Alleyoop. Body in the closet. Logan, he's..."

But before I can announce that Gus is dead, Aunt Winnie leans in and presses two fingers to the side of Gus' awkwardly bent neck. "There's a pulse!"

My own heart rate races at the good news. Relief floods me, but it is quickly chased away by the angst of wondering who would possibly do this to an old man.

Logan is a fantastic boyfriend and a good cop, but even perfection has its limits. "Charlotte, what? Did something happen at the Soup Alleyoop? Are you okay?"

"Ambulance," I insist. "Ambulance for Gus." I can't hear Winifred's fretting nor Logan's worry. I can only hear the thrum of my heartbeat roaring in my ears. "Come quick, Logan. Gus has been attacked. He's alive now, but it doesn't look good."

My palms are sweaty even as Logan promises he's on his way, and he's bringing an ambulance on his heels. I hold the device to my sternum, my lips parted with equal measures of shock and dread. I cannot believe someone would hurt a man with sparse bits of white hair.

And if they came for Gus and hurt him so horribly, will they return to finish him off?

GUS' VERY SPECIFIC DREAM

I don't know Gus. Maybe he's been at town events, but I can't say I've had a conversation with him. Plus, I'm still considered the new girl, so I haven't met everyone yet.

Being that my first encounter with Gus has him unconscious and bound, I would say things could be going better.

I'm flustered even as I put my phone down. Logan said not to hang up, but I can't very well have my phone in my hand while I untie poor Gus. So, I compromise by keeping the call going while my phone rests nearby on the floor.

Aunt Winnie's hands do their best with the knots binding Gus' wrists while I work on his ankles. He is still unconscious, but thankfully, alive.

Who could have done such a thing?

But just as my question plagues my mind, Winnie's more appropriate, "Is he going to live?" floats in the air.

Yes, more than looking for the culprit, it matters that Gus wakes up. My fingers tremble because he looks so frail. I don't want to accidentally yank the wrong way on the knot and make things worse for him. My stomach tightens as my slick fingers take far too long to make sense of the knots.

After I free his ankles, I help Aunt Winifred with the complicated knots around Gus' wrists. "My gosh, these are tight! How does this even..." My mouth screws to the side while I take out my frustrations on the knots that aren't going anywhere anytime soon.

"Scissors," Aunt Winnie suggests with tears in her eyes. "I'll go look for scissors."

Now it's a battle of this knot against my stubborn will. Gus' skin is thin, and I don't want the scissors causing damage to an already frail man. I chew on my lower lip while I tug and twist, wanting to get this series of knots undone before Gus wakes up. I don't want him to come to still bound. Poor guy looks to be in his early eighties.

While I realize it is more important to concern myself with Gus' wellbeing, I cannot help my nature which always wants to make sense of things. "Who would do this?" I ask aloud to my great-aunt when she shuffles to the open closet with kitchen shears. "How old is Gus? Eighty? Eighty-five? What sort of sick person attacks an old man?"

Aunt Winifred's tears dot her cheeks. "You nailed it: a

sick person attacks an eighty-two-year-old man." She wrings her hands, twisting the skin on her knuckles. "Oh, Gus. Don't give up. Agnes will come around. Open your eyes, hun."

I balk at her phrasing. "Agnes? What do you mean, 'she'll come around'?"

Aunt Winnie seems to realize she didn't want to have said that in front of me. "Nothing. I really don't want Gus to die, is all."

She hands me the scissors, which do their best to cut through the many layers of rope. But the stuff is thick and tough, and the scissors don't know how to be all that helpful against the fat fibers.

"This isn't kitchen twine," I tell Aunt Winnie. "This isn't something Gus would have had handy in the kitchen, even if he was roasting pork and whatnot and needed kitchen twine." I shake my head. "This was premeditated, if the attacker brought their own rope."

Aunt Winnie's hand goes over her mouth. "I can't think of a single soul who would want to hurt Gus. He's a quiet gentleman. Keeps to himself and wouldn't hurt a fly. I've never even heard him raise his voice!"

I have no medical training, so I don't know how to revive Gus, or if reviving him is a thing I should be attempting without proper backup. The most I can do is work on the rope, which I do until finally, his hands fall free.

I count the seconds until help arrives, but Gus is still

sagged against the wall, his eyes closed when the paramedics come in through the front door.

I hear Greg's squawk of surprise from the restaurant area, and then two sets of feet that come in and usher Aunt Winnie and me out of the way.

We hang near the stove, where I start cleaning up the tomato mess because I can't help myself. I am a cupcake baker, and for years, I longed for my own cupcakery where I could make inventive creations to sell to the public. Now that I have a kitchen that I use to make my dreams come true, I am extra protective of other industrial kitchens. I feel a kinship to people who have specific dreams and get to see those wild imaginings come to life.

Bill, the owner of Bill's Diner, is a grump and probably doesn't have all that many fans in Sweetwater Falls. But I don't mind his grumping. In fact, I find it amusing most of the time, because we are cut from the same cloth. I want a cupcake bakery, and he wants a restaurant that... well, that makes the worst broccoli cheese soup I have ever tasted, to be honest. But his dream for his business is specific, so I have a respect for his finicky nature.

While I don't know Gus, and have never properly met the man, I clean his stove of the tomato mess because he, too, has a specific dream for his business.

A very specific dream.

I mean a basketball-themed soup restaurant? You don't get much more niche than that.

The paramedics get Gus onto a stretcher, and finally,

he rouses. "What... How did... Winifred?" His gaze catches on my aunt. His throat sounds so raspy and dry that I itch to get him a cup of water, but the paramedics seem to be doing their thing far better than I could ever attempt it.

Winnie holds his hand while the paramedics get him situated. "We found you in the closet, Gus. Who tied you up? Who hurt you?"

My arm stills its wiping on the counter, so I don't miss a word.

"Bill. It has to be Bill. Winnie, I..." He grimaces and smacks his lips together.

My stomach bottoms out.

I must have misheard him. Bill wouldn't attack anyone. He's a surly grump of an old man, but he's not violent.

I mean, he bangs pots and pans when he's worked up, but that's not the same as hurting an actual person.

I refuse to believe it, even as Winifred gasps at the conjecture and takes it as news.

Gus' thinned white hair is matted on one side, but luckily, I don't see blood.

Aunt Winnie's tone is soft as silk. "Deep breaths, Gus. You're not going to face the Emergency Room alone. I'm going in the ambulance with you. Hold on, youngster."

"There's only room for one of you," the nearest paramedic tells Winnie and me.

Aunt Winnie turns to face me. "Call Agnes and Karen. If they need rides, can you..."

"On it!" I assure her as the four make their way to the

exit. My voice sounds weird in my ears, an octave higher than usual.

Bill? Gus thinks Bill attacked him?

No. No, it's not possible. Bill is my grumpy buddy. We aggravate each other; it's our thing. He wouldn't knock out an old man.

But as two policemen filter into the kitchen while the others are on their way out, I hear Gus again. "Bill. It might have been Bill. Whoever it was sneaked up behind me and walloped me in the back of the head. Had to be him. The letters will tell you all you need to know."

After Gus is safely tucked into the ambulance and two officers come into the kitchen, I realize I am going to have to get a better understanding of Bill's relationship with Gus if I am going to get to the bottom of what went down at the Soup Alleyoop.

NEW SOUP CHEF

*L*ogan had to go straight to the hospital, as was his assignment from the precinct since he wasn't on the detail in the area of the restaurant. After I assure him on the phone that I am just fine, he ends the call so he can do more important things, like his job.

Like proving Bill didn't hurt Gus.

I call Karen and then Agnes, informing them of the fiasco with Gus. Karen's reaction is what I would expect. She is a spritely old broad. Thin as a pole, but tougher than nails when she is determined.

"I'll bring my knitting up to the Emergency Room. And a sandwich for Winnie. It's nearing lunch time, and I know she'll be too worried to think about eating. She's got to be beside herself with this whole thing."

"That's a good idea." My mouth pulls to the side. "I don't know Gus, so I'm not sure what he needs. I don't even really know what happened. I'm out of sorts with this whole thing."

Karen's voice drops to a quiet worry. "Did you tell Agnes yet?"

"She's my next call. Then Marianne."

"Good. Don't call Agnes. I'll do it. She might fall apart, and I don't want her to be alone when she does. I'll tell her in person."

"Your golf cart is hardly something you should be driving in winter weather, Karen. I'll come pick you up."

I can hear Karen bustling around her kitchen. "Actually, your dashing boyfriend installed enclosures on my golf cart yesterday, so I can get around without having to call you or Marianne whenever I want to leave the house. I think he's going to winterize Winnie's golf cart next."

I pause through the wave of affection mingled with appreciation that settles in my sternum. "Logan mentioned wanting to fix up your golf cart, but I didn't know that's what he meant. That's so sweet."

"Indeed. He's a solid sort of gent." I hear a cupboard opening and closing on her end. "I'll tell Agnes, you tell Marianne. Poor Gus. The man wouldn't hurt a fly. Literally. I swatted at one in front of him once, and he shooed the fly out of the house instead of killing it. That's a gentleman."

My shoulders lower at the kindly mental image. "Call me if you need anything?"

"Always do, honey cake."

By the time I inform Marianne of Gus' downfall, the

police officers have finished conducting their investigation of the area, since there isn't all that much evidence to gather. Pictures are taken, they ask perfunctory questions about the state in which I found Gus, but after about half an hour, they leave without further instructions.

My mouth pulls to the side as I survey the kitchen. Should I shut down the business? Why would the police leave without closing the place down at least for the day? I mean, leaving it open like this makes it seem as if the Soup Alleyoop is open for business.

Then it dawns on me that, as I recognized neither of the officers, they might have assumed I work here, and am capable of running the business without Gus, which couldn't be farther from the truth.

I need a plan for this place. My gaze searches for a schedule that might give me the name and number of an employee who might be of some help.

There is no separate office that I can tell, only a desk in the back corner of the narrow kitchen, where a great number of papers are piled up on the cluttered surface.

Luckily, my eyes fall on the schedule, printed out and taped to the wall above the desk.

"Huh," I say to myself. "Looks like Hunter is on the schedule for this morning, but not until two."

I glance around at the kitchen.

I should leave. Even though the tomato soup mess is mostly cleaned up, this place is in no shape to open for the day and actually serve customers.

Then again, maybe it is. I am here. The menu can't be all that complicated if the entire thing is just soup and fountain drinks.

I should leave. This isn't my business. I could go right now and leave a note for this Hunter person to let him know why his boss isn't here.

But if my business was unattended and I couldn't serve my customers, would I want my kitchen closed and all that business lost?

My heartache cannot be helped when the image of Gus' face resurfaces in my mind. Such a helpless expression to match a hopeless situation.

I can't close his business and leave his customers hanging. I have no idea what state this business' finances are in, either. Maybe he needs every sale he can get. What if taking this week or so off to heal puts him in the red? What if the Soup Alleyoop has to shut down for good, and Gus heals only to come back to a business that went under because he couldn't be here to make it happen?

I move toward the industrial refrigerator, questioning every step that leads me there. I don't see recipes out anywhere, so cooking up one of Gus' soups isn't an option.

But when I open the fridge and see three pots clearly marked as leftover from yesterday, I reason I am, at the very least, skilled enough to reheat three pots of soup for the poor man, so he doesn't lose out on a day of business.

I feel like I am being sneaky, though I know I'm not doing anything but trying to help Gus when he clearly needs it. Still, rummaging through someone's kitchen is akin to rifling through a person's underwear drawer. Things are in a specific order and shouldn't be messed with if I don't have permission.

Even so, I take a leap and move the pots to the freshly scrubbed stovetop. The quiet clicks of the burners turning on feels like a scandal announcing itself to the building at large.

"I'm just heating up soup," I tell the building for no reason other than to clear my conscience.

But the simple act turns into far more than just that when two families come into the restaurant with a combined total of six noisy children.

I don my cheeriest smile and move out of the kitchen to the food counter to greet the newcomers. "Hi, Laura," I say to the woman I have met in passing several times at the various town festivals.

"Hi. Charlotte, right? Winifred's niece." Her brows pucker as she struggles for thought amid her three boys who are all vying for her attention, asking for her to rent them a basketball. "You bake cupcakes. I put in an order for four dozen yesterday. You're still doing that, right? Please tell me I don't have to make the cupcakes myself for Benji's birthday party. Kids are so finicky at five."

I hold up my hands, unsure if she can hear my response over her children's antics. One is jumping with his hands up, knocking her breasts with every hop. It's energy I am unfamiliar with and cannot match.

I smile at Laura. "I'm still doing that. Don't you worry. Today I'm just helping Gus out. He's feeling a little under the weather this morning, and I didn't want him to have to close."

"Whew!" Laura seems to be well-versed in holding a conversation while her children try to talk over us. She also seems to be able to decipher what is an emergency squawk of her name on her children's lips, and what can wait until she's had two full sentences of conversation with another adult. She angles her body away from Benji, who seems bent on jumping on his mom to use her as a jungle gym, whether she is ready for him or not. "That's a relief. I don't know if you've noticed, but I have my hands full. I desperately need the birthday desserts taken off my list."

"Absolutely. What can I get you today?"

"Three kids' basketballs, a cup of chicken noodle, two cups of tomato soup, and the limitless bowl of the Manhattan clam chowder for me."

I have no idea what anything costs, so I consult the menu behind me overhead like a novice, punching in the prices and jotting down what each person ordered, in case the scheduled employee named Hunter needs that sort of information when he gets here at two o'clock.

I have no idea what I'm doing, but Laura doesn't seem to care that I fumble through the cash register and money exchange.

Luckily, I find a key in the register labeled "Balls".

I hold the thing up. "I'm guessing this unlocks the basketballs for the kids?"

Laura smiles at me, though I can tell her patience with her children is wearing thin.

I can't say I blame her.

I glance under the counter and note that there are two glass cupboards, one marked for kids and one marked "regular".

I am grateful that the key works. I pull out three kid-sized basketballs, which appear smaller and squishier than your average court-sized ball.

The moment I hand over the three balls to the boys, they shout their glee and race to the nearest hoop. Even though there are at least a dozen hoops their size around the restaurant, they all fight over one.

Yikes.

Laura sags against the counter, her tension gone in a gust. "Thank goodness. Winter is so stressful because they can't go outside or play with their friends as often. If Gus didn't have this place, I would go insane. He's not here?"

"No, Gus is out today. I'll bring your soups to you, alright?"

She looks mildly relieved that Gus isn't here, which strikes me as strange. She exhales and dons a bright smile. "You're a gem. Thank you."

I wait on the next woman, who calls to Laura to get "the big table" for their two families.

"Hi, welcome to Soup Alley—"

But I don't finish my sentence, because the woman talks over me in a gust. "Three cups of chicken noodle and an endless bowl of the Manhattan clam chowder. Three kids' balls. Different colors than Laura's kids, so they don't fight over them." Then she rolls her eyes. "Like that'll help. Who am I kidding?" She lowers her voice. "The second her kids see the color my kids have, they'll scream until they switch. On second thought, make them all the same."

She talks fast, so I don't have much time to comment or process what she is saying. I find my feet moving to the ball cupboard and handing over three balls, which I've got to say, I am wary to do.

Six children who look to be all in elementary school, each armed with a ball?

I wonder if this job should come with a helmet.

I take her cash and promise to get her order right out.

I do not stop moving for the entire two hours it takes Hunter to arrive for his shift.

Delivering food, taking more orders, unsticking balls from hoops, reminding kids not to climb on tables, and bussing booths in between taking orders is not a one-person job.

Luckily, I don't burn any of the soups, and no giant catastrophes occur on my watch.

Though, if there is a person who can handle this amount of chaos, I don't know who that gentle soul might be.

It is definitely not me.

I like to think of myself as a mild-mannered woman. I'm decently agreeable and have plenty of pep in my step. Plus, I volunteered for this job that nobody asked me to do. I have no reason to complain.

Except that Laura's kids are absolutely wild, and they don't seem to have designs to leave anytime soon.

I don't blame her. I mean, the kids are well entertained, and she gets to sit with her friend and have adult conversation. However, I look forward to the moment when she takes her kids home, as they seem to be the catalyst for all the problems in the dining area.

I don't understand how a person can nurse the same kind of soup for two hours, but every adult who comes in orders the same thing: bottomless Manhattan clam chowder. They keep coming back for refills, so much that we are nearly to the bottom of the giant pot only two hours in.

I have never tasted Manhattan clam chowder. The tomato broth with vegetables has clams swimming around in it. Clam chowder has always reminded me of subpar broth with gross membranes floating in it that are too chewy to digest. The clams look like snails, which do not appeal to me in the least as a suitable lunch option. But I have to admit, the aroma of the soup here is pleasant.

When the pot of soup nears its end, I fear that the mothers in the restaurant will revolt. They order bowl after bowl, not slowing down no matter how many crackers I put on the side of their orders to try to fill their stomachs.

Laura is on her sixth bowl. She keeps rubbing her midsection contentedly.

When a man who looks to be a year or so out of college, maybe twenty-three or so, strolls behind the counter, I have to remind myself that hugging a total stranger simply for walking into work is not what most would consider proper behavior. "You're Hunter?"

The young man is about two inches shorter than me, but his moussed light-blond hair makes up the difference of my five-foot-ten height.

He quirks an eyebrow curiously at me. "Sure am. You're... new?"

"I'm so glad you're here." I fish around and locate the sign I have been chomping at the bit to use. When the "Back in Five" hits the counter, I heave a sigh of relief. I motion for Hunter to join me in the kitchen, where there aren't sensitive ears who shouldn't hear dark tales about the restaurant's owner.

"Hi. I'm Charlotte McKay, Winifred's niece." Hunter doesn't know who I am, but he nods in recognition at mention of my great-aunt. "Oh, right. I think I heard something like that. Winnie's the best. When I got caught out after curfew back in high school, Winnie would call my mom and tell her that I was 'helping an old lady' who couldn't figure out how to get the darn light switch working." Hunter mimics a frail woman's voice, adding a little levity to the situation.

"Yep, that's Winifred, for you. We came in this morning

when the restaurant was supposed to open, but no one was here."

Hunter rubs the nape of his neck. "Yeah. I usually open, but Gus was taking over for me because I had a dentist appointment."

There are most likely better ways to ease Hunter into the explanation, but I am just flustered enough to go straight for the bare facts. "Aunt Winnie and I found Gus stuffed in the supply closet back here. He was passed out and tied up." I pause only for Hunter's gasp and raised eyebrows. "Gus is in the emergency room with Aunt Winnie. He's alive, but he looked to be in bad shape. I didn't want his business to have to close while the doctors do their thing, so I just sort of started heating up the soups that were in the fridge."

My explanation loses steam near the end. When I say the words aloud, I worry I sound crazy. No one asked me to keep the business open, yet here I am, deciding I know what should be done for Gus' business, which I have very little frame of reference for, concerning its day-to-day operations.

I wanted to be helpful, but now I worry I have turned into a busybody who walks into random businesses and does as she pleases without permission.

Hunter's mouth falls open. "Um, yikes. That's awful. Is he okay?"

I'm grateful Hunter doesn't seem offended by my uninvited presence here.

I offer a hapless shrug. "No idea, to be honest. He was awake when they took him in, but he's not going to be in any position to come back for at least a few days."

Hunter grimaces. "I need to check on him." Then he cringes. "But I'm on the clock. Tonight, after I close out, I'll go check on him." Then another problem pops up. "There's no way I can work the restaurant on my own. The other regular employee is out of town. Gus is filling in for him." Hunter shakes his head. "That's not the thing to think about right now. Why would anyone hurt Gus?" As if he doesn't need me here for anything, his voice deepens while he answers his own question. "Bill. That snake. It's gotta be Bill."

I hold up my hands before that train of thought goes any further. "Whoa. Slow down. One headache at a time. You're the only person working at the restaurant this week now?"

"For the next three weeks, actually. Gus was going to fill in for the other guy, who goes on a wilderness hike every February." He pinches the bridge of his nose, dread plain on his face. "I guess I won't be going to my buddy's party."

I shake my head, speaking before I run my words through any sort of mental filter. "I can help out. I mean, I have plenty of experience in kitchens. Point me to the recipes and I can start cooking." When Hunter hesitates, I fold my fingers together in supplication. "Please do not send me back out there. Laura's kids are a nightmare! I know that's a terrible thing to say about children, but I'm at my wit's end with them! I didn't know kids wanted to literally try to hang from ceiling fans, but twice I had to get them down after they tried building a tower out of chairs!"

Hunter chuckles, which is a surprising response. "Yeah, they're a crazy bunch. Keep you on your toes, that's for sure. Gus had to ask them to leave last week. He didn't use the word 'ban', but that was the gist. I'm guessing Laura saw Gus wasn't here today and took her advantage." Then he casts me a look of pure hesitation. "I can handle the front desk, but Gus is real particular about who gets to see the recipes. Like, real particular. I had to sign a nondisclosure agreement before he let me see the recipes, so even if I needed the help back here, which I do, I legally can't show you the recipes."

I take a step back at the level of protection provided for simple pots of soup. "Seriously?"

"It's award-winning stuff." Hunter holds his hands up. "I legally can't show you the recipes, but if you get Gus' okay, then I would love the help this week. I honestly can't do it all alone and I'm pretty sure the parents in Sweetwater Falls would revolt if one of the few places they can take their children closes during the season they need it most. This place gives them all a break from being cooped up."

I hang my head. "I'll go back out there and deal with the front desk area and the children trying to tear the roof off the place. But the second Gus okays me being back here away from all the insanity, we're switching."

Hunter smirks at me. "Deal. I like it better out there, anyway. I get bored back here, cooking by myself."

I jot down which days I can come in to help Hunter, factoring in the time away I will need to spend running my own business. Then I take a deep breath as I steel myself to brave the wild children.

I do not have a trained ear to decipher what is a cry for help and what is a war cry meant to announce the onslaught of a game of dodgeball. Two minutes back out in the wild, and I've nearly used the word "hooligan" to describe an eight-year-old, whom I might otherwise find precious. I have to stay on my toes, taking orders and trying to keep the kids from killing each other with basketballs.

But one thought stays in my mind while Laura's kids take turns trying to hit each other in the head with their balls: both Gus and Hunter seem certain that Bill is the one who attacked Gus.

If I am going to get to the bottom of this, I will need to spend more time at the Soup Alleyoop than I was anticipating.

In fact, I will need to spend as much time as it takes in here to clear Bill's name once and for all.

4

BILL THE BULLY

While I was hoping for a quiet winter wonderland sort of week, that has quickly turned into the struggle of juggling two jobs.

I did this to myself, so I can't exactly complain when my feet hurt while I'm working all morning in my kitchen. I've been here since before the sun rose so I could get my baking done before heading over to the Soup Alleyoop to help Hunter with the afternoon shift. I usually love the silvery glow of the concrete floors. The stainless-steel counters sparkle with the dusting of sugar that always finds a way to scatter in random places around the kitchen of the Bravery Bakery.

But today, I am dragging. I don't even hum to myself when I set the mixer whirling. While I love every inch of my kitchen, I am still a little rattled from the bedlam of working the floor at the Soup Alleyoop yesterday.

Thank goodness Gus signed a release for Hunter to show me the recipes. I cannot handle the chaos of kid land a second day in a row. I signed some piece of paper, stating I wouldn't disclose his recipes, and secured myself a spot in the kitchen, where the basketballs won't be flung at my head when I tell the kids not to hang on the rim of the basketball hoop. By the end of the day yesterday, my nerves were shot.

I still can't get the accusation out of my head that Bill is at fault for the attack. While he is probably the least sunny resident of Sweetwater Falls, I just don't think he has it in him to knock an old man in the head and then tie him up.

And stuff him in a closet.

I shudder when I recall the disturbing mental image that I still haven't been able to shake.

My gaze trails to the corner of the counter, where a knitted doll stares at me with angry brows bunched.

Is it normal to have a handmade doll of Bill? In Sweetwater Falls, it's not completely strange. Last month, there was a Knit Your Heart Out fair, wherein the local book club sold their knitted and stitched wares to raise money for their club. The big reveal was that they handmade dolls in the likeness of various townsfolk, which we could bid on and take home.

I knew that when Bill's doll went on the docket, I would not be outbid.

First off, not too many people love Bill. He's an unapologetic grouch.

Second, I was just wound up enough to spend way too much on a child's toy.

I've grown attached to the cranky expression on the ten-inch knitted doll. He even has a knitted cup of his horrible broccoli cheese soup in his little hand that Agnes stitched for me after I bought the beloved toy.

Doll Bill has taken up residence in my kitchen because I enjoy having a buddy silently grouse at me while I work. I whistle happily, while, in my imagination, Doll Bill says something surly, like, "Keep it up, Cinderella. Whistling doesn't make the job go any faster. Am I paying you to entertain the customers, or to, I don't know, do your job?"

His bad attitude doesn't make him all that popular, but I never minded it. In fact, now that I am not a waitress at Bill's Diner, I get a great deal of amusement, thinking about his complaining.

When Marianne pops her head into my workspace, I am not sure I have ever been more relieved to see my best friend. "Hey, Cupcake Queen. Need a hand?"

I'm sure I look just as desperate as I feel. "Several. Thank goodness you're here!" I put down my spatula and beeline for her.

I dwarf her with my superior height, which makes her fit perfectly in my arms.

Marianne giggles at my exhaustion. "Wow. I didn't realize it was that bad. I would have come sooner."

I release her and then grimace. "I got chocolate fudge frosting on your shirt!"

RED VELVET VILLAINY | 37

Marianne snickers. "That's the thing about owning a washing machine. I don't have to worry about little mishaps like that." She tilts her head at me. "Are you alright?"

I glance down at my apron, noting how chaotic the stains are. "Honestly? I'm not sure. I'm spiraling instead of actually thinking in a straight line."

Marianne moves to the refrigerator and takes out the eggs and butter. "You caught me up on all I missed on the phone last night, but I haven't had a chance to stop by and visit Gus yet. Any updates since yesterday?"

"Winnie told me he was admitted to the hospital. Poor guy."

Marianne nods. "Agnes is with him now. Then Karen is going to go over there in the evening to relieve her." She trots to the counter. "I'm going to start making a batch of cupcakes. Which flavor do you need me to whip up? I was thinking maybe I could bring an extra cupcake over to Gus this afternoon when I stop by."

"That's a good idea. I don't even know Gus, but I feel so horrible for him. He's got one of those faces, you know? The kind that makes you want to speak softly and give him whatever he asks for, even when he doesn't ask for it."

Marianne's head bobs. "That's Gus, alright. The Soup Alleyoop is his baby. He loves those rowdy kids. Gets this big smile when he sees them, which, if I'm being honest, not many people do when they see Dennis and Laura Miller's kids coming. They're a little..."

"Wild? Rude? Uncontrolled?"

I can't believe I would ever say such hurtful things about children, but the Miller boys bring out the savage in me, I guess.

Marianne laughs as she dumps copious amounts of butter into her mixing bowl. "I was going to say 'spirited', but all those other adjectives apply."

I move back to my station and pick up my piping bag, focusing on getting the double fudge cupcakes frosted and finished. "I can't get my mind off the fact that Gus is sure Bill attacked him. And Hunter's guess was Bill, too. I don't understand. What bad blood could there be?"

Marianne snorts. "Um, I don't think Bill is anyone's favorite person." She motions to the stuffed toy on my counter. "Even his doll looks mean."

"But does the doll look murderous? I don't think so." Instead of reaching for the spatula, I throw up my hands in exasperation. "I'm not going to be able to focus until I talk to Bill. What did he have against Gus? Did they fight recently? If so, what about? What on earth might two old men bicker over?"

Marianne shrugs while the mixer whirls. "Sounds like you're in for a fun conversation with Bill. Might want to wear a helmet."

I tilt my head at her. "Hilarious."

Marianne holds up her hands. "Hey, if he's in the habit of clobbering people over the head, it just makes good sense."

My gaze fixes on the fishbowl beside Doll Bill. My gold-fish is getting bigger. Her fin flicks the water in my direction as if she hears me and cares about my conundrum. "What do you think, Buttercream? You don't think Bill is guilty of attacking an old man, do you?"

As if in response, the goldfish that Logan won me at the Twinkle Lights Festival swishes her tail at me.

"See?" I say to Marianne, who chortles at my evidence. "Buttercream doesn't believe it was Bill, either. That's evidence right there."

Marianne adds the special-made cardamom-scented sugar and then the vanilla. "I don't think a goldfish and a doll are the witnesses you will need to clear Bill's name." She peers into the mixing bowl while it whirls. "Something you will need, though, is another suspect. If you don't think it's Bill who could have attacked Gus, then who in Sweetwater Falls do you think might have bashed an old man in the head and then tied him up?"

It's a fair question, but not one to which I have the answer. I cannot fathom someone in Sweetwater Falls hurting an old man so cruelly.

But first things first: with Marianne here to help me finish up my baking, I might have time to stop by Bill's Diner before heading over to the Soup Alleyoop to get started in their kitchen.

My feet ache while I keep my eyes fixed on the cupcakes that are still in need of fudge frosting.

Yes, this is going to be a long day.

But if I'm going to get to the bottom of who hurt Gus, I'll need to ignore my aching feet and do a little poking around at Bill's Diner.

5

CUPCAKES FOR BILL

$\mathcal{M}$y time spent working as a waitress at Bill's Diner isn't anything I would like to repeat. When I walk in and Bill spots me, his thick eyebrows raise. "Oh, good. You got an hour for me, Charlotte? I need you to bus some of these tables. Becca is taking the longest break of her life. I'm barely hanging on."

My lips purse at the nearly filled dining room. "I don't have a ton of time. I actually just stopped by to bring you a cupcake and have a quick chat."

Bill throws the dishrag he slung over his shoulder at me. "Chat while you bus. That's the deal. And I'm not selling your cupcakes at my diner, if that's what you're getting at by bringing me that thing. I sell pie, and that's that. I don't need the fancy stuff. People like their pie just fine."

I narrow my eyes at him. "I brought you the cupcake because you're my constant bucket of sunshine, not for any ulterior reason."

Except that I brought it to coerce him into answering my questions so I can cross him completely off the list of suspects.

My plan is not swimming along, as I had hoped it might.

I set the small box with the cupcake down and start in on bussing the nearest tables, so they can have decent turnover today. Just because Becca seems to be the only waitress on the clock this morning doesn't mean she deserves to have customers mad at her because she couldn't seat them soon enough.

The tables I start in on are laden with half-eaten meals, which is quite different than the soup bowls at Gus' restaurant. Those were practically licked clean, while the plates here still have plenty left to pick at. The oldies station plays overhead, reminding me of the countless hours I worked here, clocking out stinking of French fry oil.

I really thought my days working at Bill's Diner were over. But after my fifth table bussed, I know Bill is about to ask me to do another chore.

Thankfully, Becca returns from her break.

"Would you look at that!" I say to Bill with enough extra cheeriness to make him blanch. "Looks like you have some time to talk with me after all. Lucky me."

Bill grumbles at Becca, not because she took a long break, but because she took a break at all.

"Sheesh!" she offers in my direction, voicing her frustration with Bill as she pulls her shoulder-length hair into a ponytail. "Whenever the other waitress calls off, I get a double-portion of his attitude."

I have to stop myself from offering to wait tables to help Becca out. I remember what it was like working here when I was the only waitress holding down the fort.

But I already have a job to get to that isn't my own.

I really need to stop doing that.

I wish Becca luck and scoop up my small box with the single cupcake inside. Then I trot into the kitchen, prepared to corner Bill.

"Not so fast, Mister. You said I could talk to you if I bussed tables."

"You've got one minute."

I squint at him, matching his attitude with some of my own. "Actually, I bussed five tables, so I get five whole minutes. Them's the rules."

Bill grumbles as he makes his way to me, banging a pot on his way. The aggressive sound makes the cook flinch.

That doesn't bode well for me trying to prove Bill's innocence, but I don't let that stop me.

"Did you hear about Gus?" I ask, starting in slow.

He crosses his arms over his chest. His bulbous nose sniffs, and his mid-fifties weathered skin has a sheen of sweat to it. "Your little boyfriend stopped by this morning to ask me about the last time I'd seen Gus. Did you want me to have this conversation twice?"

Drat.

I pull myself up, trying to match his stature that is a few inches taller than mine. "Being that Logan can't discuss police business with me, yes. That's exactly what I'm asking. Gus seems to think you attacked him. I don't think you did, so I'm here to make sure I'm right: that you're a jerk, but you're not about to knock Gus out like a maniac."

Bill throws his head back. "You realize I took a chance on you and gave you a job here, right?"

I swallow hard. "Right." I motion to the space between us. "You realize that this little detour doesn't count as part of the five minutes of conversation you owe me in exchange for bussing those tables, since you're clearly dodging my simple question."

Bill runs his tongue over his top row of teeth. I'm not sure if that does anything to keep his vitriol inside, but I'm hoping this might be the ticket to getting an actual answer out of my former boss. "You think I hurt Gus?"

"No, I think you didn't. But Gus seems to think you did. Tell me why Gus would assume that."

Bill sizes me up, as if trying to ascertain whether I am worth his confession. When he finally speaks, I am ready for either the truth or more of his sass. He throws up his arms that are disproportionately longer than his pooched belly. "Look, Gus and I don't see eye to eye on a few things, and we got into it. But I didn't hurt him. I yelled at him a little, only because he didn't see a good opportunity when it looked him in the face. But that's all. We argued. I wrote him a letter with my proposal, which he never responded to after the first time he told me no, and that was that. Gus can run his business into the ground, for all I care. I was trying to do a good thing for the both of us, but he was too muleheaded to see it."

I do my best to attach only to the relevant parts of that conversation that still need clarifying. A hiss fills the air when the cook throws some bacon fat onto the griddle behind us.

"What business opportunity did Gus pass on? And why did it make you mad enough to yell at him? Gus seems like a sweet guy."

Bill offers up a noise that sounds like "pfft." "Just because someone sounds nice doesn't mean they have good sense. He runs the soup place, right? I have a perfect soup I wanted him to put on his menu for a share of the cost. My broccoli cheese soup is fantastic. Everyone orders it. I wanted him to sell it at his restaurant and we could split the profits. I could even make it for him and deliver it. But Gus said no. Says his recipes are his own, and he only sells dishes he makes up at his place." Bill scoffs, as if I should be able to clearly see how ludicrous that standard is. "Can you believe that?"

Um, yeah. I can't completely believe that Gus would

pass on Bill's offer. Bill's broccoli cheese soup tastes like burnt rubber. And the broccoli is such a small portion that it's barely a sprinkling. It gets ordered so often here because out of towners frequent the diner, and also because that is the only soup on the menu.

Bill's soup is dreadful. I can understand why someone who goes as far as having nondisclosure agreements drawn up for his own recipes might not want anything to do with Bill's inedible swill.

"You two had an argument, and that's that?"

Bill turns his chin, so he doesn't have to look me in the eye. His bushy brows lower, making him look exactly like the knitted Bill doll in my bakery's kitchen. "I sent him a proposal in the mail, along with a strongly-worded letter that he needed to reconsider. It would have been good for the both of us. Gus isn't getting any younger, you know. He could use my help, making one of his soups so he has one less thing to worry about. He's getting up there in years. He needs to start thinking of the future. I could help him. Stubborn old fart."

I blow my breath out before responding. "Define 'strongly worded'."

Bill rubs the nape of his neck. "I may have called him shortsighted, which he is. I may have told him to watch his back if he ever decides to put a broccoli cheese soup on his menu, because this town already has the perfect one being sold at my restaurant." Then he narrows his eyes at me. "I did not hurt him." He wags his finger at my glare. "If you want to talk to someone who might have more of a reason to be cross with sweet old Gus, ask Laura Miller. Her boys were banned from his restaurant after they broke one of his basketball hoops."

My nose scrunches. "I highly doubt a mom would assault someone over being asked to leave an establishment."

Bill shakes his head, chuckling with irony, not humor. "You've never seen a mom who needs a break as bad as Laura Miller. That place is one of the few in the cold months where she can turn her monsters loose. You obviously haven't met her kids if you think a mother wouldn't resort to violence if someone took away her precious break from those three." He motions to the kitchen. "You ever see those three kids in my diner?"

My mouth pulls to the side while I think about it. "No, I can't say I have."

"That's because the Millers know I don't tolerate those hooligans in my establishment."

I frown at Bill. "Can you really do that? I mean, they're just kids. Kids make noise. They're messy. It's part of the gig."

Bill holds up his hand. "I don't mind normal kids. It's her kids that are terrible. I won't let them in. The last time they were in here, they ran behind the counter and pulled down the coffee machine. Could have been a serious lawsuit."

I lower my chin as I glower in his direction. "You mean

someone could have been seriously injured. That's the important part, right?" I scold him.

"Yeah, yeah. Either way, I blame Gus for not putting my broccoli cheese soup on his menu, not for kicking out Laura's kids. If you want to aim your pesky questions at anyone, I would start with Laura Miller."

I harrumph. "Well, you don't have to sound so smug about it."

He raises his nose sanctimoniously. "Yes, I believe I do."

I purse my lips, glaring up at him. "You know, just for that, I'm going to stand here and watch you eat this entire cupcake that I made for you. It's delicious, and I know you'll hate it. You like that terrible broccoli cheese soup, so you wouldn't know quality food if it jumped into your mouth, which this cupcake is about to do if you don't eat it."

Bill's upper lip curls. "I'm not eating that thing. Cupcakes are for children."

"Yes, and right now, you are acting like a giant child." I open the small box and take out the gift I made him.

When he turns up his nose at my offering, my temper flares.

"Eat this stinking cupcake, Bill."

"I only eat the food I make at this diner. It's delicious, and you don't know what you're talking about. My soup is award-winning."

Becca trots into the kitchen, mopping her brow with a napkin. "It's packed out there, Bill. I need your help."

I scoff, knowing Bill's claim to fame has to be a lie. "That terrible soup of yours has never won you any award."

Becca snickers. "No kidding. It's gross."

Bill scowls at the both of us. "It's award-winning, I tell you!"

I throw up a hand in exasperation. "What possible award are you talking about?"

He looks down his nose at me, indignant. "My Soup of the Month award. Every month, it wins."

I have just about had it with Bill today. I should leave while I still have my dignity and self-control intact.

But I'm just tired and wired enough to act on impulse, letting my frustration get the best of me.

Instead of putting the cupcake in the box, I take the thing and smash it to Bill's curled upper lip. "There! It's my award-winning cupcake. In fact, I think Bill's Diner just awarded me Cupcake of the Month, since it's the only cupcake in the building!"

I march past Becca and stomp out of the kitchen, leaving the scandal of my childish outburst behind to the tune of Becca's giggles and vehement whooping.

No, Bill is not my favorite person, but I still don't think he hurt Gus. Now I have to track down a harried mother and see if I can figure out if she is the one who put Gus in the hospital.

The visual of Bill's chocolate-smeared shocked face dances in my mind's eye, even as I drive off to the Soup Alleyoop, where hopefully the Miller boys won't torment their mother to her breaking point.

6

CHEF CHARLIE

*I*f I thought my recipes were inventive for my cupcakes, they don't hold a candle to Gus' soups.

"Am I reading this right?" I ask Hunter, who peers over my shoulder at the notecard, which is splattered with dried tomato soup. "Yeah, and you don't want to skip that step. Part of why Gus trusts me to make the soups for him is that I don't cut corners. If it says stir it fifty-seven times, don't stir it fifty, or fifty-eight. He's got a system, and it's flawless." Hunter holds up his hands as if I am about to pepper him with protests. "I don't make the rules, but I have no problem following them if it's Gus."

Hunter's light-blond hair is coifed in the front again, giving him an extra three inches of height. He tugs the black-and-white striped referee uniform over his head and then loops his whistle around his neck. "It's so weird to have someone else back here. Usually, it's just me, Gus and the other guy." He tilts his head at me appraisingly. "You know, I don't mind you in our space. That's high praise."

I snort at his humor. "I'll try not to faint from the swell of your admiration." My mouth pulls to the side. "Gus doesn't measure the clams by weight or volume? He counts each one?"

Hunter nods. "I'll show you. You have to count them, otherwise you might get subpar ones that are destined for the trash. His Manhattan clam chowder is the money-maker. Ever wonder how he can charge so much for the bottomless bowl?"

I take out a giant pot from the cupboard below. "I did think thirty-five dollars for bottomless soup was a little steep."

"People will pay it without blinking once they take a single bite. They pack it away, mind you, but they come back over and over for the soup. Sure, the basketball gimmick is good to keep the kids amused, but the parents stay so long for the soup. I've seen kids be ready to go home, but the parents make them stay longer, so they can have another bowl."

I laugh at the mental image of a parent craving a soup that bad. "I've never cared for any sort of clam chowder, but I know how to follow a recipe—even one as detailed as this."

"Thanks, Charlie. I really would be up a creek without a second person here. I would have to close the doors, and

I know Gus wouldn't want that. Winter is his busiest time. It's the stellar soup combined with one of the few indoor activities available in the cold months for kids."

"Charlie?" I question him with a smile.

Hunter grins at me. "I think it suits you."

"I'll take it."

Hunter and I exchange a fist-bump before he goes out to open the doors and greet the actual line of parents congregating outside in the snow, waiting to come inside.

I have two pots of soup already on the burner, which should be ready in the next five minutes. It's this clam chowder that is starting to look more like alchemy than actual cooking.

But I keep my head down and don't question the system. Hunter came in early and made a pot of the stuff already, so I have time to get this one going. But I know it's going to take me a good hour to follow these instructions.

I can do this.

Marianne calls me while I am partway through chopping the carrots in the exact shape he specifies. It's not a clean dice, nor is it a julienne. He wants the carrots diced on the bias, so each cube is on an angle, instead of the sides being straight up and down.

"Can you believe Dwight turned in his book late, and then tried to act like *I'd* made the mistake and misfiled it? I mean, honestly. If you're going to lie about a dime in late fees, you have too much time on your hands. And then I have to decide if ten cents is worth me going to the mat because I know I am right, and Dwight is trying to get out of paying his paltry late fee."

I snicker at Marianne's frustrating work conundrum. "These are the drawbacks of being Head Librarian at the most beautiful library that ever was. You have to deal with the Dwights of the world."

Marianne sighs, and I can picture her in the old church building with stained-glass windows and steepled ceiling, surrounded by tomes of her favorite stories. "The library is beautiful, isn't it?"

"You sound like you're reading. Anything good?"

"Not good. Amazing. Have I ever told you how much I love Charlotte Bronte? It's the language combined with the no-holds-barred plot twists. She is my kind of girl, and I love it." Resentment sneaks into her tone. "I'll bet Charlotte Bronte wouldn't have let Dwight lie to her face. She wouldn't then apologize for the fabricated mix-up to the man. She would have said something witty that put him in his place."

"You didn't apologize to Dwight for the mix-up, did you?"

Marianne harrumphs. "I can't help myself! See? This is the problem with being a nice person. I apologize without realizing it. Before I can stop myself, the words are coming out of my mouth. Being nice is the worst. I'll bet Gus knows my pain."

I start cutting the celery in the same way: not quite a clean dice, but dicing on the bias. I make piles and piles of

RED VELVET VILLAINY | 55

slanted celery cubes while Marianne unburdens herself to me.

"Speaking of Gus, Agnes is upset," Marianne informs me. "I mean, we're all upset that Gus is hurt, but she was sniffling when I called her half an hour ago. Said she's to blame for the whole thing."

My knife stills. "How's that? Agnes didn't assault Gus."

"I have no idea. It was weird. Then she quickly changed the subject. I might stop by her place tonight after I close the library. Maybe I'll bring her a book to calm her nerves. Not this one, obviously. Charlotte Bronte is not for the nights you need comfort and solace."

"I guess this is the wrong time to tell you that I've never read anything by Charlotte Bronte, so I have little frame of reference for what you're talking about. Is that like, *Emma*? Or *Sense and Sensibility*? Because I saw one of those movies a long time ago, but I don't remember the details. I don't recall it being disturbing, like you're suggesting. Maybe the book is different from the movie."

Marianne groans as if my literary ignorance pains her. "Charlotte Bronte wrote *Jane Eyre*, *Shirley*, and countless other stories that make you question if there is still hope in the world."

"Well, then definitely don't send one of those to Agnes if she's upset."

"You share the same first name. You need to get better acquainted with this author, Charlotte."

I chuckle at her logic. "Well, when you put it like that."

Marianne's voice quiets. "Charlotte, why would Agnes think Gus' accident was all her fault? I've been trying not to ask myself that, but I can't stop the question from popping into my head. Agnes didn't... I mean, obviously Agnes would never hurt a fly."

I barely give Marianne's fretting a second of credence. "I wasn't on the phone, so I don't know how she sounded, but I cannot imagine Agnes is the culprit. Like, I physically can't picture it."

Marianne sucks in a deep breath. "Me neither. I don't know what she meant, but it can't be that."

I set to Gus' next step in the recipe, which is to "Julienne the onion so fine that you can see straight through it, like glass."

I really hope this recipe turns out. These instructions are very particular.

"We'll find out who hurt Gus, Marianne. I stopped by Bill's Diner this morning to ask him a few questions, since Gus and Hunter both seem to think he's behind the sneak attack."

"How did that go?"

I don't mention shoving the cupcake in Bill's face. I still can't believe I did that. Bill just so happens to bring out the worst in people.

"I still don't think it's him. Bill wanted Gus to sell his broccoli cheese soup at the Soup Alleyoop, and Gus refused. Then Bill sent a rude letter to Gus, putting him smack at the top of the suspect list." I shake my head at the bad timing of it all. "Silly Bill."

"I love that you can say things like 'Silly Bill' when he is still at the top of your suspect list. None of what you just said took him out of the running, by the way." I can picture Marianne's dainty nose scrunching as the rest of what I said dawns on her. "Bill actually thinks his soup is good? He can't be that delusional. And I really can't picture a world in which Gus would entertain something polluting his brand. Everyone knows Gus has the best soup in town."

"How did I not know this?"

"Well, you've never lived in Sweetwater Falls in the winter, which is prime soup time. Plus, Gus doesn't ever compete in town events. So, he doesn't make soups for the Knock Your Soup-Off competition."

I chortle over the onions, even though my eyes are starting to water. I've chopped only one onion so far, and I have twenty to go. "The... what?"

"The Knock Your Soup-Off," Marianne repeats, as if she hasn't just said something totally strange. "It's the soup competition in Sweetwater Falls that happens in March every year. Bill always enters his broccoli cheese soup to win, and surprise-surprise, it never gets the golden soup pot."

I snort at the scenario. "Gotta love Sweetwater Falls. Why doesn't Gus compete, if soup is his thing?"

"He's a purist. And he doesn't want to win. I asked him one year, and he said that he doesn't want to take the competition and make anyone else feel bad. And he would totally win, you know. Are you making his recipes right now?"

"Trying to. Not sure I'm quite the chef that Gus is, but I'm giving it my best elbow grease."

Hunter trots into the kitchen and flags my attention. "Hey, Charlie, I could use a hand out here. Rowdy mothers. You know how it is."

I truly don't, but I end the call with Marianne after promising her again that Agnes can't possibly be the scoundrel in all of this. "How can I help, Hunter?" I ask him as I step out of the kitchen on his heels.

My mouth falls open as I survey the scene before me. There are at least three dozen children in the restaurant. While the main eating area is mostly separate from the game area, I can see by the way the mothers are guarding their bowls of Manhattan clam chowder that they are worried an errant basketball will come flying their way.

While many of the kids are shooting hoops and enjoying their time in a normal manner, there is a cluster of chaos forming in the center, where the friendly game of basketball has mutated into a rough round of dodgeball.

My feet carry me to the center when a little boy who can't be more than six gets bashed in the head with a regulation-sized basketball. He bursts into tears as both his mother and I rush to extract him from the madness.

Hunter is tooting on his whistle, but the referee uniform seems to hold little weight at the moment.

While I do my best to be careful with the little ones, corralling them to the side so they can escape to their parents, Hunter all but chucks the older kids toward the booths to get them to calm down. He blasts on his whistle, looking like a man on a mission as he hoists one of the Miller boys over his shoulder. He grabs another around the waist and pins the kid to his hip. He marches to Laura Miller, who is shoveling spoonful after spoonful of soup into her mouth, because she knows her minutes at the Soup Alleyoop are numbered.

I can't even bring myself to feel frustrated with her, knowing that it was her three kids at the center of the mess. Compassion wells in me because I can see her sheer overwhelm, and the defeat on her features because her haven is being stripped away.

I don't know anything about parenting. All I have to measure it against is owning a goldfish, which I'm guessing isn't a fair comparison. I can't judge her, as some of the other parents are clearly doing—casting Laura looks of shame concerning her children's behavior. I don't know her life, her struggles, her family.

In fact, I've lived in Sweetwater Falls for months, and I can't say I've had more than a two-sentence passing exchange with the woman.

The moment the three Miller boys have been extracted from the play area and their family's ban reinstated at the decree of Hunter and his silver whistle, the entire place calms down.

The kids go back to shooting hoops. The mothers go back to devouring the soup that I need to work on replenishing. The background stadium music playing overhead returns to my awareness.

My heart goes out to Laura as she hangs her head upon her exit with her three sons, who are shoving each other on their way out. I catch her eye and tap my heart twice, casting her the friendliest expression I can manage so she knows I see her pain and frustration.

My compassion is a stark contrast to many of the other looks thrown her way.

I catch sight of moisture pooling in Laura's eyes as she nods to me, and then exits to the tune of one of her son's loud farts.

No, I don't know what it is to be a parent, but I do know that Laura is going to get a surprise delivery of something yummy this evening.

Hunter bumps my fist, heaving a sigh of relief as his whistle dangles around his neck. "Thanks, Charlie-girl. It should calm down now."

I go back to the kitchen and continue following Gus' recipe, wondering if Laura has any friends who care that she cried today.

I work for several hours with the Millers occupying my mind. I don't even realize it's closing time until Hunter trots into the kitchen and congratulates me on surviving the shift.

"Have I mentioned I appreciate that you're here?" he

says as he surveys the many pots of soup he doesn't have to stay late to make.

I manage a tired smile. "Only once or twice. I really don't mind. I usually work only in sweets, so this is a nice educational stretch for me."

Hunter moves to the stove and lifts the giant pot for me, storing it in the fridge for tomorrow's orders. "I'm glad there's enough of the clam chowder left for me to take a bowl to Gus."

I tilt my head to the side, holding the fridge door open for him while he moves the second pot for me. His muscular forearms look like he did rowing or something like that in college. Good that he puts his muscles to use in the kitchen, where they are surely needed.

"You're visiting Gus tonight?"

"Sure am. I know he's my boss, but he's also like a grandpa to me." Hunter takes off his whistle after I close the refrigerator door. "He gave me my first job in high school and let me come back to it every summer when I came home from college in between semesters. I got my degree in accounting, but honestly, I don't see myself working anywhere else. I'm happy here."

"I think that's nice."

Hunter chuckles at my assessment. "I wish my parents felt that way. They're more than a little disappointed that I'm not putting my degree to good use. They don't get that I'm doing exactly that here."

"Accounting the basketballs?" I joke.

Hunter smirks at me. "No, smart alec. I handle the books for Gus. He taught me well enough, and college filled in the gaps. When a guy came by to franchise the place last month, I was the one who looked over the contract for Gus and saw the holes in the offer."

My eyes widen. "Wow. I didn't realize Gus was interested in franchising."

"He's not. But he's a nice guy, so he took the man's information and the offer to look over. He handed it straight to me and never gave it another thought. He doesn't want an empire. He wants to make soup and watch kids have fun. It makes him happy to be surrounded by cheering and laughter. He likes watching kids work towards a goal and then get there." Hunter folds his arms over his chest and leans his backside on the counter, a wistful expression softening his features. "I came here when I was a little guy, hoping to shoot for the high hoops. Gus used to pick me up so I could dunk. Best feeling in the world when you're little—soaring through the air toward a basketball hoop."

I hold Hunter's tender childhood moment in my heart. After a long day of work, it's nice to have a conversational connection. "Gus sounds like a good man."

"He really is. I know he's sad, being away from all the kids for so long. I'm going to stop by the hospital tonight and bring him some soup so I can tell him the highlights of the day. He'll be happy to hear that Marvin finally made a basket."

Because I am tired, my observation comes without filter. "You're not a bad guy, Hunter."

He shoots me a wry look. "Is that the city girl way of saying I'm nice?"

My head bobs. "It sounds like you and Gus have a lot in common. You're taking note of the kids' victories, just like he does. You care about the integrity of the soup, just like Gus."

Hunter's smile pulls to the side as his chin dips in reverence. "That's pretty much the best compliment you could give me, Charlie. Telling me I'm like Gus?" He shakes his head. "I can't think of a better life goal."

I drag a rag over the counter one last time, swiping up the last of the mess I made in the process of cooking. "Okay, if you say one more precious thing, I'm going to burst into tears. I've been working since five this morning, so I'm not strong enough to be diplomatically stoic when you say stuff like that. You're a good person, Hunter. I'm glad you've found happiness here."

Hunter hands me my purse. "Thanks, Charlie. For what it's worth, I'm glad you're here, too."

I tug on my winter jacket while Hunter zips up his. "I like working in the kitchen. I didn't realize you had to make the soup the day before and let the flavors sit overnight. See? I'm learning new things all the time."

He places the to-go bowl of soup for Gus in a bag, but before I leave, something tugs at my heart. "Hey, can I buy a cup of soup before we head out?"

Hunter chuckles at my question. "You don't have to pay for the soup when you're working here. That's one of the perks. I keep thinking I'll get sick of the stuff, but I never do."

I make quick work of ladling out a cup in a to-go container, but the savory soup is not for me. As much as everyone raves about the Manhattan clam chowder at this place, I still can't bring myself to taste something with clams in it.

No, this bowl is going to someone who will appreciate it.

Though my feet are aching, and my energy is waning, I know of a weary mother who needs this soup more than I do.

7

SOUP AND SYMPATHY

Finding Laura Miller's address wasn't an issue. Karen knows everybody, so all it took was a phone call to the wry and spirited member of the Live Forever Club. But standing outside the Miller's large colonial as the snow falls in the evening light, I begin to question my choice to come here.

It's not that I don't think Laura will appreciate the cup of soup, nor do I assume she will turn up her nose at my offer of friendship.

It's that even with the door closed, I can hear her three sons yelling and throwing things inside the house. It takes more than a little determination to lift my hand and press the doorbell.

Can they even hear it above the racket? I'm not sure a woman has ever needed a cup of soup and a break more than Laura.

When the door swings open, the second oldest of the three boys, who looks to be around age eight, belches out a surprisingly eloquent, "Can I help you?"

I should be grossed out, and part of me probably is, but I am more impressed that I was able to understand him through the echoey burp sounds.

"Um, yes. Is your mother home? I'm Char—"

But I don't get out my full name before the boy yells over his shoulder. "Mom! Mom! Some lady is here."

Then he holds up a finger and takes in a deep breath.

I can tell he is steeling himself for greatness, so I pay due deference to the effort he is summoning.

The kid does not disappoint but proceeds to conduct a conversation with me in solely burp-speak. "She... is... coming... Mom...is...doing...dishes."

I applaud as best I can without tipping the cup of soup.

By the time Laura comes to the door, I learned that the boy's name is Marvin, that he is, in fact, eight-and-a-half years old, and that he can also do a stellar armpit fart symphony—a skill I never mastered or, to be fair, attempted.

I can hear the other two boys bickering in the background. "Hi, Laura. I'm..." But when one of them starts angrily yelling, I switch from telling her why I showed up on her doorstep to something a bit more urgent. "Is Dennis home?"

"Yes. Did you want to talk to him?"

I shake my head and reach out, tugging on her sleeve.

"Good. Then he can be with the kids for a few. Grab your jacket and come for a walk with me. You need a break."

Laura's eyes widen. "Really?" Then scandal takes over her features as a smile finds her weary face. She calls over her shoulder in much the same way her son summoned her, "Dennis, I'll be back in ten!"

Then she shoves on boots and tugs on her jacket. She practically skips out of her house and slams the door shut, heaving a sigh of relief.

I giggle at her clear need for this simple walk as I hold the cup of soup aloft. "This is some of the Manhattan clam chowder from the Soup Alleyoop. I thought you could use something comforting and delicious."

She takes my offering and hugs it to her chest. "Seriously? Charlotte, you are my angel of mercy. Thank you!"

I jerk my chin to the sidewalk. "Feel like a walk?"

"I feel like a break, so yes. A walk sounds great." She sets the cup of soup inside the mailbox for safekeeping and steps off the porch with me onto the snow-covered driveway.

"I'm sorry things went south at the Soup Alleyoop today," I offer. "I have no idea how hard it is to be a mother."

That seems like a good opener, and apparently, that's all that is needed to get Laura to open up.

"It's impossible, is what it is. They're three rowdy boys, and there's no end in sight. The Soup Alleyoop is one of the few places open in the winter where the boys can get out and move around." She pauses for a breath, but then keeps going. "I know what all the other mothers think of me. I see their looks. They think I'm a terrible mother because my boys are out of control. They don't have to tell me my boys are difficult; I already know that. But no matter what I try, it doesn't work. Every day, I'm just hoping for a few minutes of sanity." Then she turns her chin to me. "Which thankfully, you brought me."

I cast her a sympathetic smile. "My pleasure."

It's a lovely evening walk, lit only by the reflection of the twilit moon off the snow and a few porch lights. The snow is two inches deep, and more is falling. It's the perfect place to air one's grievances.

The snow is quiet and promises not to tattle on Laura for having frustrations.

"I don't know what to do," Laura admits. "It's hard to have a social life at all. It's impossible to have people over. The boys are so wild; we can't get through a dinner without someone throwing food or spilling their drink. It used to be embarrassing, but now it's just doom." She starts talking with her hands. "Doom that I'll never have friends. Doom that I can't leave the house without fearing my boys will break something when they're out in the wild. Doom that I can't go to the bathroom without a war breaking out in the next room."

"My goodness, that sounds stressful." I wish I could offer something more helpful, but I'm sure she's heard it all.

Laura nods. "My mother gave me bath salts two Christmases ago. My New Year's resolution was to use those bath salts. To make time to take a relaxing bath once a month." She holds up her hands. "That's all I wanted. Once a month, a quiet bath moment. You know those commercials that show those women de-stressing in the tub? They have their e-readers and maybe a candle lit. They have bubbles in the tub, and I'll bet they have bath salts."

I snicker at the image I can conjure without much assistance. "Yeah. Those sorts of commercials always make me want to take a long bath, too."

"That was two Christmases ago. Do you want to know if I even cracked the seal on the jar?"

I wince. "I'm guessing not so much?"

"You guessed right. My mother got me another jar this year, so now I feel the pressure."

"Did she get you a night of babysitting so you could actually use the bath salts?"

Laura snorts. "My mother can't handle the boys any better than I can. Then with her, there's the added guilt that comes after she tries to watch them. I didn't do enough. I don't use consistent discipline. I'm not strict enough." She rolls her eyes. "It doesn't matter how strict I try to be; my boys don't listen to what I have to say. They outnumber me."

The snow falls on a particularly lovely evergreen, making it look like Christmas, smack in the swing of February.

"Are the boys any better with Dennis?"

Laura shoots me a wry look as if I should be able to guess the answer to that question. "Dennis comes home from work and checks out. He eats dinner, watches television in the basement and I deal with homework, shower time, bedtime and the like. It's not my best life."

I try not to be frustrated with Dennis before having a proper conversation with him, but I'm inching in that direction. "I wish you had support," I say, instead of blaming Dennis outright without him being here to defend himself.

Laura chuckles derisively. "I can't even be mad at Dennis. I'm more jealous that he gets to check out and I don't." She shakes her head at the situation. "I didn't use to be like this. I was prom queen, you know."

My eyes widen, as I didn't realize she would dig this far back in her memory for a shining moment to choose to hold high. "I was always put together. Never left the house without my hair braided and my teeth flossed."

I kick at a thick patch of snow as we walk on the pavement together. "I think I've always been the standard once-a-week flosser, so you've got me beat there."

Laura's eyes aren't focused, like she is seeing herself in days past. "I was a cheerleader, too. Good grades. Always put together and organized." Her expression falls as her present reality crashes back into her awareness. "I don't know how that all slipped away, but here I am, getting kicked out of a children's play place twice in one month."

She puts her hand over her mouth. "I can't remember the last time I flossed. Probably around the last time I took a bubble bath."

Compassion wells in me. "Oh, Laura. I can't imagine how hard it is for you."

Laura looks to be in her forties, so I know she is digging deep for happy memories if she's going as far back as high school for something to lift her spirits.

"When was the last time you and Dennis had a date night?"

Laura scoffs. "My memory doesn't go that far back. We lose every babysitter we ever have. We try to go out, but usually we don't get past the salad course before we have to come home because the sitter is ready to tear their hair out."

I need to get in the habit of thinking things through before I volunteer myself, but I feel myself jumping in at the sight of her floundering so hopelessly.

I nudge her elbow with mine. "I know we're still new to each other, but I wouldn't mind watching the boys for a night so you and Dennis can get out and reconnect."

Laura stops walking and turns to me. Emotion glistens in her eyes in the moonlight. "You don't mean that. Take it back, or I'll say yes."

I hold up my hands, knowing I should heed her advice. "I might have to call Marianne for backup. Fair warning: it's been a hot minute since I've babysat."

Laura surprises laughter out of me when she throws

her arms around my shoulders and squeezes tight. "Yes! Marianne is fine. Of course. The National Guard is fine. Oh, Charlotte, I can't tell you how much I need this." She pulls away with tears sliding down her pink cheeks. "I haven't seen my husband's face on a date in… It's been too long, that's for sure. I haven't been able to enjoy a meal uninterrupted in years."

Regret washes over me the second she accepts my offer, but I can't very well renege now. "It's no trouble. How does Friday night sound? Go out for dinner and a movie. Even though Valentine's Day isn't for another week or two, make it an early Valentine's Day date. Get dressed up. Floss those teeth and braid that hair."

Laura catches a laugh in her hand. "I can't believe you're offering this. Thank you, Charlotte. I didn't use to be this bogged down. I don't know when life spun so out of control, but I do need help in the form of a babysitter. Thank you. Truly."

I nod, linking my arm through hers. "What are new friends for?"

Laura lowers her head, her breath syncopating. "Thank you. Normally people see me drowning and look the other way." We take a few more steps together before we come to the end of the sidewalk and have to turn around. "Thanks for seeing me."

I give her arm a little squeeze. "Any time."

8

THE MILLER BOYS

I regret this. Before the night has even begun, I regret telling Laura I would babysit her children. I don't know what I'm doing with well-behaved children, much less the three Miller minions.

I was going to beg Marianne to help me, but before I could ask her, Marianne told me how excited she was that Carlos was taking her ice skating at the high school, where apparently that's a thing you can do.

I really need some sort of a schedule for this town if I'm going to experience everything.

I didn't want to make Marianne cancel her date, so I decided to show up without her, armed with only a few books I checked out from the library that seemed age appropriate for the boys.

As I stand on the porch, rallying my gumption so I can ring the doorbell, I am convinced this was a terrible idea.

I inhale a long breath and ring the doorbell, donning a smile that lies to the world and announces that I am not the least bit intimidated by the hours stretched out before me.

When Laura opens the door, she is beaming. "I'm so glad you didn't cancel!" she sings to me while something crashes in the background.

"Of course not. Laura, you look beautiful!"

She is decked out in a red dress that looks fit for going to the opera or somewhere extremely fancy. Her hair is in a tight French braid that shows off the hues of her makeup, which I can tell she is glad she took the time to do.

Laura leans in and smiles at me, purposefully showing off her teeth. "See? I flossed, so you know I'm serious about tonight."

I give her an appreciative whistle as she escorts me inside.

Laura hands me a piece of paper with several numbers scribbled on it. "Here's the pediatrician, the neighbor next door and my mother, just in case. Allergies are listed at the bottom. I know you're dating Logan, and it's fine if you have to call him to help you out. Or anyone, really. I'll have my phone on the entire time. Dennis is..." It's then I hear the garage door opening next to the house. "That's him! Dennis is just getting home from work. He's going to shower and change, and we'll be out of here. Did I say, 'thank you'?"

"You did, and I'm happy to do it."

That's an obvious lie, but we don't know each other well enough for her to notice.

Dennis doesn't greet her or come into the main area of the house. I hear the clinking of his keys on a counter and then footsteps going upstairs.

I'm guessing he is ready to get going on this date, too.

Laura takes the few minutes and shows me around the house. It's a nice colonial, with a large family room that is overrun with toys and dirty dishes. There isn't a spot to sit anywhere on the sofa, because the laundry is there, waiting to be folded.

I can see the plans for a design, where knickknacks of angel figurines are high on shelves, but it's clear Laura doesn't get much of a say in how the house is presented.

The boys are throwing a football from the living room into the kitchen, shouting at each other to throw it harder.

I take a steadying breath while Laura escorts me into the kitchen, apologizing for the chaos.

"Have the kids eaten dinner?" I ask, unsure if I should feed them, or if that job is already done.

"They don't sit down to eat. Believe me, I've tried. Their plates are at the table, and they pick at what they want throughout the evening. Bedtime is at eleven o'clock. Whatever they don't eat by then gets dumped."

I recall having a strict eight o'clock bedtime through most of my elementary years, but to each family their own, I guess.

Laura gives me a peek into the basement, which looks

to be largely a toy den with an old couch and a television in the corner.

I'm guessing that's where Dennis disappears to, since I see several posters on the wall for the local college football team.

By the time we come up the steps to the living room, I know Laura is antsy to leave. "I'll grab my purse, and then Dennis should be down here and good to go." She grins at me. "I'm so excited! Again, I'll have my phone on the whole time. Even if you only make it an hour, I really appreciate this. I've had this dress for three years, yet I've never worn it out of the house. I can't believe it still fits!"

I shake my head. "No. Turn your phone off. I mean it. If I have a question, I can call your mother. If there's an emergency, I have the name of the restaurant you are going to, so I can call the restaurant and have them page you. I don't want you to be worried or distracted. You just enjoy your date tonight. You deserve a night off, Laura."

Laura makes a show of taking out her phone and turning it off, exhaling as if that simple act is the sweetest relief.

When one of her children cries out in anger, her shoulders slump. She calls the boys into the kitchen to get to the root of the problem before things turn bloody.

To avoid the chaos, I migrate to the living room, where Dennis is just now trotting down the steps toward me.

Though I do not know this man well, I hold up my

hand, my nostrils flaring when I see he is clad in ragged jeans and a sports hoodie. "No."

Dennis is taller than me, older than me, I'm betting far stronger than me, but I hold firm to my sudden authority on his outfit. "Excuse me?" he asks, his brow quirked.

I motion for him to turn around, then I give him a light shove up the steps. "Your wife is wearing a gorgeous red dress. You are not wearing that. Go back up there, and don't come down until you are wearing something that requires a tie and preferably a suit jacket. Bonus points if you put on cologne."

Dennis glances back at me, brows raised. "Are you serious? She dressed up?"

"Way up. Don't blow it, Sailor. Pretend it's your first date, and you're trying to make a good impression. Pretend I'm going to throttle you if you don't come down looking like the prom king she deserves on her early Valentine's Day date with you."

Dennis groans. "We're doing that? This is our Valentine's Day? I didn't get her anything. It's not for a month still."

I glower up at him. "We're in the first week of February, pal. Now, march. And make it snappy. Beautiful women who spent who knows how long getting ready don't deserve a date who shows up sloppy and late without a gift."

Dennis quickens his pace, thank goodness. "I'm going, I'm going."

I feel my great-aunt's vinegar in my blood because I have half a mind to tear him a new one for attempting to take Laura out while wearing a hoodie.

I mean, honestly. Logan and I aren't fancy people, yet he always looks presentable, like it matters to him that I showed up.

I stand at the base of the stairs for the entire five minutes it takes Dennis to change into the appropriate suit and tie. When he comes back down, I note that he is even wearing cologne.

"Better?" he asks me, motioning to his attire.

"Much. We will not speak of your first attempt. Now go wow Laura and show her a good time. I can stay as late as you like, so dinner and."

"Dinner and?" he questions.

"Dinner *and* a movie. Dinner *and* a walk. Dinner *and* ice skating. Dinner and. She deserves the 'and'."

Dennis straightens his tie, looking far sharper than he did just minutes ago. Perhaps he is finally aware that he is actually going on a date.

When Laura rounds the corner, she looks harried, for sure, but also beautiful and still perfectly put together.

Dennis' intake of breath tells me I was right to push him back up the stairs so he could properly prepare.

Laura's flabbergast is just as notable. "You're wearing a tie," she remarks, clearly impressed, her voice soft with emotion.

She deserves a man who wears a tie just for her.

Dennis adjusts the thing like a toddler. "It's too tight," he whines, marring the dapper image.

I elbow him in the kidney. "A gentleman doesn't complain about his tie when his date is wearing heels, put on makeup, did her hair and dressed herself up in something as nice as that gown."

Dennis swallows hard. "I mean, you look amazing, Laura." As if exercising a muscle he has not used in years, he proffers his elbow to her. "Shall we?"

Laura blushes—actually blushes—when she takes his arm.

I stop Dennis on his way to the door. "Phone."

"Oh, right. In case anything goes wrong with the boys."

"No, Dennis." I will remain firm on this one rule. "Turn your phone off. That's the final piece of the date. Then you're ready to go."

Dennis nods while he complies. I can tell he is intrigued by the idea of having no distractions for one entire evening.

When the two finally make it out the door, I am relieved they are properly set up for a lovely night out.

I, on the other hand, have a long evening ahead of me.

I roll up my sleeves and march into the living room, where a squabble between the brothers has already broken out.

9

BABYSITTING BLUNDERS

To say that I am not the most experienced babysitter is an understatement. I babysat a few times in high school, but that experience did not prepare me for the chaos that is the Miller boys. They look identical, just in various stages of growth, with reddish-blond hair like their father's, and thinner lips like their mother's. But those smiles occur in the midst of chaos, so I can't appreciate the joy as others might.

I need backup, and not just because they are throwing couch cushions at each other and I now can't find one, but because it has been only half an hour, and I am tempted to call Laura to come home.

No. I will not break. I have to give Laura and Dennis a night out, or Laura will spiral further downward.

Not on my watch.

I call Logan, but he doesn't answer, most likely because

he is working late. I debate calling the Live Forever Club, but I hesitate because, as spry and lively as those ladies are, I don't want to subject them to this.

The second my phone connects with Marianne's, I feel a meatball ping off my temple, leaving a slimy mess down the left side of my face. "I'm sorry, I'm sorry, I'm sorry," I start, knowing I am interrupting her date.

Marianne laughs at my greeting. "Do you always start phone conversations like that? What's wrong, Charlotte the Brave?"

I duck when another meatball is flung my way. "My bravery! That's the problem. I thought I could handle babysitting the three Miller boys, but I can't! They're ganging up and... Ouch!"

I rub my arm where a spoon hurled at me and bounced off my bicep. I narrow my eyes at the youngest Miller boy. "Benji, you know throwing things at people hurts them. Use your spoon for eating your soup." Who knew a five-year-old could have such a good throwing arm?

"But I hate soup! This tastes like poop! Poop soup! Poop soup!" Then little not-yet-six-year-old Benji picks up the bowl and dumps it over onto the table, smiling as the red tomato soup spreads out in a wave across the surface.

I clutch the phone to my ear. "I will give you my first-born if you let me cut your date short so you can come over here and help me survive this night!"

Marianne's laughter cannot be contained. "On it.

Carlos has fallen three times on the ice. I'm sure he could use a break. Is it okay if I bring him?"

"Yes! Bring him. Bring the National Guard! Help me!"

Marianne snorts at my desperation and then ends the call.

By the time Marianne and Carlos get to the Miller's house, three bowls of tomato soup have been dumped over —one of which splattered all over me. My shirt was purple and cute when I showed up to babysit. It went nice with my dark-washed jeans. But as neither garment is salvage-able now, I suppose the outfit won't be separated even when it finds its new home in the garbage tonight.

There are now no couch cushions anywhere to be found. I don't know how they did it, but the couch cush-ions have vanished, and Marvin, the middle child, is jumping on the springy base of the couch, launching Lego bricks throughout the living room like little missiles of mayhem.

The coffee table in the living room has been tipped over so Nathan, the oldest, can position himself behind it and use the thing as a shield while the Marvin throws Lego bricks at his brother.

Nathan is armed with shoes and boots, which keep hitting the wall behind the couch with a horrible thud.

I throw open the door, my eyes wild. I hold myself back from hugging Marianne, as I am still dripping with tomato soup. "Thank goodness! You're a good friend. I owe you so much for this. Carlos, I'm sorry I..."

But I don't get to properly apologize to him for ruining his date with my best friend, because a loud crash sounds behind me.

I wince, afraid to turn around.

Carlos steps inside, his eyes wide. "Oh, wow. Charlotte, you weren't kidding."

Marianne stands in the foyer, where she can glimpse the chaos of the living room and measure it against the mess in the kitchen. I don't know that my sweet, soft-spoken friend can do anything to put a stop to the madness, but either way, I have backup now.

Carlos moves into the living room and extracts Marvin from tackling his older brother, who has finally come out from his coffee table shield. "Which one is this?"

"That's Marvin," I tell him. "Marvin is supposed to be doing his homework, but I can't get him to sit down." I wring my hands, horrified that I let the evening devolve to this. "I can't get anyone to do anything!"

Carlos salutes me without an ounce of judgment for me or the children. "I've got Marvin, then." He marches the eight-and-a-half-year-old to the counter in the kitchen and sits him down after righting one of the fallen stools. "Tell me what homework you have, Marvin."

Marvin responds by tilting his rear end toward Carlos and farting in his direction.

I should have warned Carlos that might happen, as that's the response I got when I asked Marvin to sit down and eat his dinner.

At least it's not just me who can't get them to settle down.

When the youngest sitting at the kitchen table starts tipping over glasses of water to add to the tomato mess, and Nathan starts throwing shoes at the wall, since he doesn't have Marvin to assault anymore, my sweet best friend decides she has had enough.

With two fingers on the sides of her mouth, Marianne lets loose an ear-piercing whistle—a sound of which I did not know she was capable.

Everyone stops and stares, gaping at her because no one can match Marianne's volume—not even the Miller boys.

Marianne smiles at her captive audience. "Benji, you've earned yourself a bath. Wait for me in the bathroom, and I'll help you." Then she turns to the oldest child in the living room. "Nathan, you get to be my assistant, so start by lining up the shoes next to the front door. If one is out of place, I'll know."

My mouth drops open because the boys actually start falling in line. Nathan picks up the shoes and begins lining them up beside the front door like a good little soldier.

How did she do that?

At Carlos' behest, Marvin moseys to his backpack and dumps the crumpled contents onto the counter beside Carlos, who inhales with determination at the disorganization. I have seen Carlos at work, and I know such chaos makes his insides itch. Yet he keeps his voice light and level while the two work on sorting through the mess.

Benji leaves a sticky red trail all the way from the kitchen to the first-floor bathroom, where he calls to Marianne, "I'm here!"

"How did you do that?" I ask her in sheer wonder.

Marianne casts me a wary look. "It only lasts for like, ten minutes, so act fast. Can you take care of the kitchen mess while I get Benji cleaned up? And then deal with Nathan after the shoes are lined up?"

I nod. For the first time in an hour, I can hear the sound of my own voice without the backdrop of kids shouting. "Yes, but how did you get them to listen to you?"

Marianne talks to me over her shoulder as she makes her way toward the bathroom. "I'm the scary librarian." Her brows waggle mischievously at me, leaving me with the mystery of how she came to wield such power over the rudderless.

Carlos takes the pages scattered across the counter and begins to sort them into piles beside a hapless Marvin. "Okay, we can start with this page. It looks like it was due two days ago."

Marvin shrugs. "Then I don't have to do it. I'll only get half credit. What's the point?"

Carlos fixes Marvin with a fatherly face. "If your teacher assigns it, then we do it. Your teacher put time and effort into making this assignment so you could learn the material. Do you know why your teacher did that?"

"Because she's mean?"

Carlos shakes his head without a hint of irritation at the sass. "No, because she cares about you. She wants you to learn and grow, so we're going to do every assignment she has ever given you, whether you get credit for it or not. If she shows up for you, then you will show up for her."

Marvin slumps atop his stool. "Half credit for late work is a stupid rule."

"Half credit is better than no credit. Not doing an assignment on time isn't a way to get out of doing work. Here's your pencil. Let's start with the first question."

His even temper and patience make him a perfect match for Marianne, and a solid friend for me. I wanted to do exactly that with the boys—check their homework—but I haven't been able to get one single thing accomplished.

Perhaps babysitting is not my forte.

10

CROWD CONTROL

I turn to the kitchen to face my doom, now that I have the brain space to focus. The tomato soup ocean is all over the kitchen table and the floor, so I waste no time getting on my hands and knees after the tabletop has been dealt with. I go through about half a roll of paper towel in the process, but it is a worthy sacrifice to pay for a non-tomatoed kitchen.

My knees are sore from being on all fours on the hard kitchen floor, cleaning up the mess. The inside of my nose stings from the cleaning solution that is doing its best to keep up.

Laura has to deal with this every day? I would drown my sorrows in Gus' soup, too, if I didn't have Marianne and Carlos here to help.

Carlos is a fountain of patience as he talks the unmotivated Marvin through his homework. He doesn't show even a hint of frustration when the boy starts whining. The undone worksheets keep piling up the more Carlos investigates the backpack.

It takes me three rags and more paper towel than I can quantify to get the rest of the kitchen wiped down. Then I set my sights on Nathan, who still has not lined up the shoes. Instead of completing the simple task, he has taken it upon himself to attempt juggling a sneaker, a slipper and a boot, which is going about as well as one might expect.

I am just testy enough to snatch the slipper out of the air before it crashes to the floor once more. "I don't think this is what you were asked to do."

Nathan sighs. "Oh, fine. But how else am I supposed to teach myself how to juggle?"

I soften at what looks like actual eagerness rather than petulance. "I can teach you. Or rather, I can learn alongside you. But I don't think shoes are the thing we start out with. First things first: we need a juggling area. That means these shoes need to be lined up and out of the way. Then we need to clear out the living room. See all those toys? If you want me to teach you how to juggle, we need absolutely nothing on the carpet. It inhibits dexterity."

I have no idea if any of that is actually true, but I can't stand to trip over one more toy.

Nathan nods eagerly. "Okay!" In no time at all, the shoes are lined up.

His enthusiasm drops, however, after two toys are

picked up off the floor. "Forget it. I don't need it perfectly clean. It's clean enough."

I shake my head. "I'm telling you; all the best jugglers have a clear workspace. This is serious business."

We work together, putting toys into the ironically empty toy basket in the corner of the living room until everything is picked up. I fold the blankets and stack them on the end table beside the cushion-less couch.

I narrow an eye at Nathan. "Find the couch cushions and put them where they belong."

He rolls his eyes at me, as if I've earned that sort of attitude. "Marvin had them last. Make him put them back."

"Marvin is in homework purgatory. Find them, or I'll get Marianne out here to do her whistle again."

Nathan scowls at me but goes to the basement and brings up the cushions. He throws them on the couch's base, which is not what I asked him to do.

I cross my arms and stare at the haphazard cushions expectantly. "I think you can do better than that."

Though, truly, I'm not sure I believe my own words.

He manages the feat with a layman's effort.

"Good. Now we can learn how to juggle. Can you find me four oranges or apples?" I ask him, guessing that's a good place to start.

While he hunts in the kitchen, I take it upon myself to dust the coffee table and the shelf along the wall, realigning the picture frames so Laura can actually enjoy looking at them. I even manage to get the scuff marks from the shoe-launching war off the wall.

By the time Nathan returns, he has three oranges and a cup of applesauce.

I frown at the offering. "We'll see how far we get with that."

I take out my phone and locate an instructional video on learning how to juggle, which holds his fascination for the duration of three whole minutes.

Our first attempt is lackluster, but after ten minutes of picking up oranges off the floor, we manage a decent offering that sort of resembles juggling.

"Hey, you're not half bad at this. I mean, we only just watched that video, and you've thrown and caught and did the juggling thing for five whole rotations. I don't want to get ahead of ourselves, but this might end up being your thing."

Nathan grins at me, looking truly proud of himself. "Really? You're not just doing the grownup thing where you say 'good job' but you don't really care?"

I smile at him and shake my head. "I really mean it. Let's master two oranges, then see how we do adding a third."

He nods so fast, he looks like a bobblehead doll. "I can do it."

I can tell this is the thing Nathan has been wanting to learn for quite some time. It is the only thing that has held his attention for more than a passing glance.

I love this. If this is babysitting, then I love it. Everything up until this point has been borderline torture, but this is a true connection.

Plus, I'm slowly learning how to juggle, which is an underappreciated talent. I plan on showing off to Aunt Winnie the second I get home.

Which won't be for hours.

I cheer Nathan on, reminding him of the helpful tips we learned in the juggling video. "Remember your focal point. Don't get distracted by the movement."

He is doing fantastic. I mean, truly impressive for this being his first time juggling, but when I hear Marianne's voice call to me from the direction of the bathroom, Nathan fumbles, dropping both oranges onto the floor.

"Charlotte, could you bring me an extra towel?"

"Sure thing." I hunt down the linen closet and get her what she needs to dry off the sopping wet child, and now soggy bathroom. When I return to the living room, Nathan looks mildly spooked, his eyes wide as they dart toward Marianne's whereabouts.

"Everything okay?" I ask him.

Nathan doesn't answer right away. "You invited the witch into our house, you realize. That's the only reason I'm doing so well with juggling."

Whatever I expected him to say, it was not that. I tilt my head at the preteen. "Huh? What witch? You're doing well with juggling because you're working hard, and you took the time to educate yourself first. That's a recipe for success."

Nathan whispers with a note of desperation to him. "Scary-anne Marianne the Librarian. She's a witch."

I press my lips together to fend off a giggle. "What? Where are you getting your information?"

He replies with the frustration of one who has to explain the obvious points of life to someone too naïve to warrant patience. "The library is haunted. Have you seen it at night? There are lights flickering in the parking lot because of the ghosts."

I love everything about this story, so I sit on the couch and get comfortable because I want infinitely more of this. "Tell me all about it. I never noticed."

"Everyone knows her library is haunted. That's why we only go there in the daytime."

I nod, as if this all makes sense. "Thanks for the heads up. But I've got to say, I think you're just plain good at juggling. I don't think Marianne cast a spell on you."

"Think what you want; I know the truth. I've never been able to juggle before, even though it's been my life's dream. Scary-anne Marianne the Librarian walks into my house, and suddenly, I'm the best juggler in the state."

Man, I love how kids think.

I lean in. "Then let's take advantage of her being here and juggle our hearts out."

Nathan takes my advice, nodding emphatically. "Okay!" He goes back to juggling two oranges, building up a rhythm until he can go an entire minute without dropping anything.

It's actually pretty impressive.

After Marianne takes the freshly bathed Benji up the stairs to his bedroom to tuck him in for the night, Nathan and I watch the tutorial video again, so we remember how to incorporate the third ball into our juggling rhythm. That seems to be the tricky part.

I didn't care if I ever picked up this hobby before, but tonight, Nathan's determination is contagious. Now I *need* to learn how to juggle.

Even an hour later, after Marianne and Carlos put Marvin down for the night, Nathan and I are still at it.

I hold up my hands when Carlos hangs Marvin's newly organized backpack on the hook near the front door. "You guys, you guys, sit down and watch this. I swear, it's the coolest thing you'll see all day."

I wait until Carlos and Marianne are seated in the freshly cleaned living room, and then nod to Nathan.

The twelve-year-old boy looks nervous, now that Marianne is in close proximity, but after a bolstering nod from me, he inhales deeply and starts juggling with three oranges.

Not two.

Three.

Carlos and Marianne are transfixed, their mouths agape. Carlos begins clapping to match the rhythm of Nathan's throws, while Marianne's hands do a little dance midair.

It takes three whole minutes before Nathan loses his count and drops the oranges to the floor. Marianne and Carlos cheer for him, marveling at how impressive his new skill is turning out to be.

I taught a kid something.

The feeling of pride fills my ribs. I can't believe I made an actual connection with a kid.

I can't believe the Miller boys didn't burn the house down on my watch.

I smile at Nathan. "You have to show Gus what you can do when you go back to the Soup Alleyoop," I tell Nathan. "He'll be so impressed."

Nathan shakes his head. "Mom said we're never going back there. She and Gus had a fight."

Marianne catches my eye, a glint of suspicion and intrigue entering her features. "What kind of a fight?" she asks him.

Nathan shrugs, taking a step away from the town witch. "The kind where they went into the backroom at the Soup Alleyoop and I could hear her yelling all the way through the place."

Marianne leans forward. "When was this?"

The boy shrugs but doesn't answer. I can't decide if he just has no idea when it happened, or if he won't answer because it's Marianne who asked, and he is afraid she might turn him into a frog or something.

Marianne locks her gaze on mine. "Your mother has a lot on her plate. I'm sure it was nothing."

Nathan shakes his head. "I know all the phases of Mom's yelling. There's 'I'm overwhelmed' yelling, which is like, here." He raises his hand to shoulder level, indicating a moderate volume. "Then there's what I heard at the Soup Alleyoop that day." He raises his hand to his forehead, letting us know that Laura really blew up at Gus on that fateful day. For what reason, I can only guess. "All I know is that when I yell like that, I get in trouble. Must be nice to be an adult. You can lose your temper and not get grounded."

I pick up the oranges from the floor. "What was she upset about?"

Nathan looks away. "Gus said we had to leave. It wasn't me. It was my brothers. Sometimes they're a little wild."

Carlos scoffs but covers it by feigning a cough.

Yes, it's only the other two who are wild, and never Nathan, I'm sure. I just scrubbed shoe scuff marks off the living room wall because he's an angel of a boy.

I was hoping to cross Laura off my list of suspects, but it seems that if she followed Gus into the kitchen and could be heard yelling through the restaurant, she might have had motive to hurt the old man.

Perhaps she came back when the restaurant was closing down. Maybe she sneaked into the kitchen, since she'd followed him there once before.

Maybe she crept up behind him and bashed him over

the head to get back at him for humiliating her with the ban he placed on their family.

My shoulders lower as defeat washes over me. I don't want Laura to be the kind of person who attacks an old man—verbally or physically.

After Marianne and Carlos leave because the house is finally under control, I go back to helping Nathan incorporate the third orange into his juggling repertoire until we've got it down.

But all the while my mind is focused on what exactly Laura was yelling at Gus about, and how far did their argument go.

Is it worth attacking an old man for a slice of sanity?

11

AGNES AND BERNARD

*A*gnes has been a no-show around the house lately, which isn't like her. Karen and Agnes are always coming and going, which is how I prefer it. I love seeing their smiling faces. I collect far more cheek kisses when there are three of them milling about.

But when I asked Aunt Winnie this morning where Agnes was at, since I hadn't seen her in a couple days, Winnie lowered her chin over her morning tea. "Agnes isn't quite herself these days. She's hiding out, I'm guessing. Gus went home yesterday from the hospital, but he still doesn't know who attacked him. She's quite upset about the whole thing."

"Were they close?" I asked Aunt Winnie while I fixed her a coddled egg with toast.

Coddled eggs. She's the cutest.

I have been asking questions like that for days, but

finally, Winnie opened up the smallest amount. "I think you should go visit Agnes today. Bring her a cupcake and see if she'll open up about it. It's her story to tell."

It wasn't in my plan to visit Agnes after I baked my heart out in the kitchen of the Bravery Bakery this morning and then pulled a shift at the Soup Alleyoop, but if Agnes is upset, I want to be there for her.

She knitted my favorite cardigan, after all.

After I help Hunter close down the Soup Alleyoop, I drive over to Agnes' house while talking on the phone with Aunt Winnie.

"I think the party is going to be just fine. The town decorations go up tomorrow, so that will get everyone in a festive mood."

My hands hurt from chopping several pounds of vegetables in the meticulous way Gus prefers them, but I do my best to keep my hands at ten and two while I drive through the snow-laced town. "I should have guessed that Sweetwater Falls would go all out for Valentine's Day. I feel bad that I'm not helping." My shoulders slump. "I'm not helping with the town decorations. I'm not helping with your party. I still don't have a cupcake flavor of the month yet!"

Aunt Winnie chuckles at my frustration. "Might that be because you're saving Gus' restaurant from closing while you're running your own business?"

I harrumph. "Sure, but that's no excuse. I want to have fun with you."

Winnie's smile is harder to hear. "I'm afraid the girls and I aren't much fun these days. I've thought about cancelling the party, but I suppose I shouldn't punish the whole town for what some horrible person did to Gus."

My brows knit together. "I can't believe there's still no progress on that front. I haven't talked to Logan today. I'll ask him if he knows anything when I see him next, which will be..." I pause because I have no idea when I will see my boyfriend. Had I not crashed my best friend's date, I'm not sure when the next time was that I would have seen Marianne. I'm glad I get to help Gus. It was my idea to step in. I guess I didn't think it all the way through, though.

Aunt Winnie's voice is filled with compassion. "Gus should be back on his feet in a few days. Hopefully your days will open up, and you'll be able to blush at that cute boyfriend of yours on a regular basis."

"Fingers crossed."

"You're on your way to see Agnes?"

"Sure am. Just pulling into her driveway now."

"Tell her I love her. Call me after and let me know if I should come by to be with her."

There is definitely more to Gus' story than I am aware of, because not once have I heard Agnes mention Gus, yet Karen and Aunt Winnie have made it sound like Gus' incident has torn out her heart.

In truth, I've been avoiding Agnes, though I've been so busy working that I have unintentionally avoided everyone in my life. But when I overheard Agnes telling Winnie that

Gus' incident was all her fault, I knew I should get as far away from that information as possible. Sure, I want to get to the bottom of who hurt Gus, but not if that person is Agnes.

Could I turn in the woman who kisses my cheek and brings me cookie dough when I'm sad?

I know I'm not that strong.

I end the call and turn off the engine, readying myself for a mix of comforting and interrogating my sweet friend.

Those things tend to go better with frosting. I am armed with one of my vanilla latte cupcakes with a butterscotch buttercream frosting to offer up, which I know Agnes likes.

I don't often get to see Agnes without her makeup. I also don't regularly see her clad in pajamas that look as if they have been worn all day. But when she comes to the door looking like she is in desperate need of a hug, I'm glad I made visiting her a priority.

"Oh, Agnes," I say in lieu of a greeting. I come inside and wrap my arms around her. "I heard you were having a rough moment, so I'm here to drink tea and eat cupcakes until life doesn't seem so hard."

Agnes chortles sadly at my plan for the evening. "I might not be very good company."

"I might not leave even if you kick me out."

Agnes kisses my cheek and ushers me inside her ranch-style home.

Unlike Aunt Winnie's home, there isn't a touch of

mauve anywhere in sight as we walk through the living room to her kitchen. Agnes' décor is centered around collecting hundreds of little figurines of lighthouses. Most of her furniture is a soft blue, with plenty of knitted blankets to accent the nautical theme.

I pull out her chair for her at the small, round table in the kitchen, and then set about fixing tea to mend her broken heart.

"I'll start brewing while you start talking. I want details, young lady." I wind my arm through the air to get her started. "Let's vent all the sadness. No sense keeping it locked inside."

Agnes smiles at me. "Well, I guess I don't have a choice, do I. You're strict."

"You're depressed, so them's the rules."

Agnes' shoulders slump. "I suppose I am more than a little sad. Gus is... This whole thing is horrible. I mean, Gus is a good man. The sweetest in town, really. To think someone would purposefully hurt him is just..." Then she shakes her head. "But I did it. I hurt him."

I freeze, hating that this is the second time I've heard her confess to the crime. "How's that?"

In the back of my mind, hearing her profess to Winnie that she was guilty of hurting Gus was something that I know should have spurred me onto asking more questions. I should have dug deeper and put Agnes at the top of my list of suspects.

But part of me knows that even if Agnes did bash Gus over the head, I wouldn't have the strength to turn her in.

I love the Live Forever Club, and all they represent. Without them, I wouldn't have opened the Bravery Bakery. I wouldn't be nearly as open to taking chances as I am now.

I wait out Agnes' silence, because if she is about to tell me she attacked Gus, I am not sure I will know what to do next.

Finally, Agnes speaks. "Gus has a... I don't even know how to say it."

I will myself to muster up enough patience not to jump on her words. "Go on. I'm listening. I'm here all night, Agnes. As long as you need."

Or, I can at least stay until four in the morning. Then I have to head to the bakery to get cracking on the orders.

Agnes seems to be taking me at my word because she goes silent again. The minutes drag on for what seem like forever until she finally begins to unburden herself.

She fiddles with the lace on her pajama gown sleeve. "Gus is a sweet man. He's been... I don't know for how long. Two years? Three? Gus writes me letters."

I have no idea where she's going with this. Still, I listen until more starts coming to the surface.

"Just nice letters about his day, asking about mine and whatnot at first. But then they turned into... I mean, calling them love letters sounds... I don't know." Her cheeks pink. Agnes looks all flustered, not meeting my eyes while she picks at the lace on her sleeve. "I was married for thirty years, Charlotte. I know it wasn't cheating on my late husband to receive those letters. I know Bernard would want me to be happy. But I couldn't do more than read Gus' letters. After a few months of that, I started writing back. Oh, it's silly. We live in the same town. I could just go over to his business and take him out for a date. But I don't know how to do that. Oh, I can go skydiving and dancing and whatnot, but dating?" She shakes her head while I pour the hot water. "That's a risk I don't know how to take."

My lips purse as I set our steaming mugs on the table and take the seat beside hers. "We'll get back to skydiving later, because I'm not sure that's the best idea. But dating? I didn't realize you felt that way. Do you like Gus enough to date him? Maybe we should start there."

Agnes blinks at her mug as her lower lip quivers. "I love him." Then she shakes her head. "But I don't know how to do that. I slept next to the same man for thirty years. I don't remember how to date. I don't know what I'm doing, so I haven't done a thing, other than write him letters." She cups her hands around her mug. "Such poetry, Charlotte. You have no idea how gallant a man can be, even when the woman is undeserving."

"Undeserving?" My nose crinkles. "Where did you get that idea?"

She sniffles. "He took a risk. He started writing to me. He deserves someone who won't shy away from something wonderful. I want to be brave, Charlotte, but this is different than breaking and entering, or putting sugar in someone's gas tank."

Gotta love her examples.

"Whose gas tank did you..." I shake my head. "Never mind. You love Gus, but you're nervous about taking that leap and acting on it?"

She bunches the flannel fabric over her chest. "I can't fall in love again. It was too hard when Bernard died. It took me years to recover. I can't go through that again."

I have no frame of reference for losing one's spouse. I cannot fathom how horrible that experience was—and no doubt sometimes still is—for Agnes.

But I do know fear. I have an intimate relationship with anxiety and shutting up when I should be waving my flag and making myself known.

I cover her soft, wrinkled hand with my own. "Agnes, I can't imagine how hard it was to lose Bernard. But if it were me in your shoes, I think I know what advice you would give me."

Agnes sniffs and then meets my eyes. "I would tell you that life is for the living, and love is for the taking." She purses her lips as she digests her own advice. "I don't know how to be brave. Not with this."

I shake my head and sit back in my chair. "Actually, I think you don't know how to live in this limbo of fear. That's why you're so unhappy. I think you're good at being brave. The longer you sit in this in-between space, the deeper your misery is going to grow. The waters are deep, and that's scary." I lean toward her. "But you know we'll catch you."

Agnes nods, a look of concern penetrating her rounded features. "That's very true." She tucks a white curl behind her ear.

"Who caught you the last time? When Bernard passed and the waters were too deep, how did you stop drowning?"

"Karen and Winnie, of course. And Marianne. Really, everyone. They set up a meal train for me. Made sure someone was in my house at least once a day for months after Bernard passed. They were good to me even when I refused to package up Bernard's things. They saved me."

I sit up straighter. "Are Bernard's things still here?"

Agnes nods, looking a mix of ashamed and sheepish. "I know I need to let them go. There's no reason to keep them. He's not coming back."

It's not said with any insecurity, but rather with a resigned statement of the facts.

I stand and hold my hand out to her. "Show me."

Agnes takes my hand and leads me to her bedroom, where again, I am greeted by lighthouse figurines and a large painting of a seascape that stretches at least four feet high. It's beautiful, just like Agnes. I'll bet she painted it herself.

Her bedspread is the color palate of a summer sunset, and even though I can tell Agnes isn't feeling her best self these days, the bed is still perfectly made.

She opens the closet and shows me the third that is still occupied with Bernard's things. Old man shirts with mostly short sleeves and faded beige patterns hang in perfect rows as if they are still waiting for Bernard to open the closet and select one for the day.

A short sob catches in Agnes' throat. "See? How can I date a man when I still have my husband's things in my closet?"

I run my hand over the men's shirts, and fish one out at random. It's a long-sleeved white dress shirt with thin sky-blue stripes running down the length. "This is a nice one. I'll bet he looked real dapper in it."

Emotion glints in Agnes' green eyes. "He absolutely did. There wasn't much the man didn't look good wearing." She pulls out a second shirt and sets it on her bed. "Maybe it's time to be brave," she whispers.

Without needing clarification, I set the shirt in my hands atop the other, and add more to the pile at a pace slow enough to match Agnes' as she takes down three more and sets them on the bed.

I am respectful with Bernard's things, and even go so far as to give each item a hug before I add it to the growing stack. I'd like to think that if I'd known Bernard, we would have been fast friends.

I mean, we both love Agnes, so that's an easy topic to bond over.

I wonder if he would have taken me fishing or hunting, or whatever it is he was into. I wonder if I would have hated the adventure, or if I would have enjoyed stepping out of my comfort zone because he made it fun.

All I know is that Agnes loves Bernard, so I love him, too.

I didn't come over here with the goal of packing up her late husband's things, but it seems that this is what Agnes needs tonight, so I am more than happy to help her however she likes. We are quiet as we take out his clothes, hug each one and set it on her bed. Occasionally she smiles sadly at a garment, and I can tell she's thinking of a memory that is too precious to give voice to.

After we take his clothes out of the closet, the shoes follow. Then the things in his dresser, which leads me to ask quietly if Agnes would like Bernard's dresser removed from the house.

I keep thinking Agnes will eventually get decision fatigue, but it's as if the moment she was willing to part with Bernard's first shirt, everything else fell into place.

Even though it's late, Logan picks up when I call. "Hey, Miss Charlotte. You alright? You don't usually call after nine o'clock."

I keep my volume quiet while Agnes takes Bernard's clothing out of his dresser. "Could I bother you to come over to Agnes' for a bit? I need help moving a dresser. I'm helping Agnes take Bernard's things out of the house."

Logan doesn't need convincing. He offers up his muscle and his truck, even bringing over boxes so we don't have to hurt Agnes by stuffing Bernard's things into garbage bags.

We work in near silence, packaging up Bernard's possessions and moving them into the back of Logan's navy pickup truck.

It's a good man who is worth holding onto for this many years after his passing.

It's a good man who lets you call him at nine o'clock at night to come help a friend.

By the end of the night, Agnes has relegated a small number of Bernard's things to keep, which all fit in the storage portion of her ottoman. She can pull them out and hold them as often as she likes, but she won't be confronted with them at every turn.

The entire process is quiet, respectful and done at a pace of Agnes' choosing.

After Logan drives Bernard's things away, promising to take them to a veteran's resale shop, Agnes finally breaks down in tears.

My arms go around her so I can hold her together as best I am able. "You did it," I praise her, hugging her tight. "And look! You took a big leap, and I am right here to catch you. Those were some deep waters, Missy, but you did it."

"I did it!" It's only then that I realize her tears are partially due to joy and triumph, not just grief. Agnes shudders in my arms and squeezes me tight with a sigh of relief I can tell she has been waiting to release for years. "I was brave."

12

AGNES THE UNSTOPPABLE

My soul is still buzzing from the swell of emotion I experienced last night while helping Agnes pack up her late husband's things. I stayed the night in her house, sleeping in the guest bedroom, in case she experienced any sort of whiplash of regret from the purge.

But when my alarm rings at four in the morning to remind me to start my day at the bakery, Agnes gets up with me, oddly alert and peppy. She whistles as she fixes her oatmeal in the kitchen. She even adds a little extra brown sugar to her meal with a scandalous gleam in her eyes. "I think today should be blessed with brown sugar."

I raise my glass of orange juice. "Today and every day, Agnes the Unstoppable."

I didn't put much more than a few seconds of thought into the new nickname, but it sure suits her perfectly.

Agnes is amazing, and can tackle anything she puts her mind to. Unstoppable is exactly what she is to me.

"Could you help me fix a couple sandwiches, Charlotte?" She sits down and straightens her spine with clear pride. "I think I might pay my favorite poet a visit this afternoon. Gus won't know what hit him when I show up with a lunch for the two of us, all dressed up and fancy." Then she blanches at her phrasing. "Poor choice of words. I wish I knew who hit him."

I smirk at her bout of bravery. "I think getting dressed up for the man who writes you love letters is just the sort of thing today needs. Might want to make sure he's sitting down when you tell him you'd like to start dating. I can't believe you put him on hold for two or three years."

Agnes chuckles. "Me neither. But that's all over now. I'm not going to hold myself back anymore. I'm Agnes the Unstoppable." Her round chin lifts with pride, and I love it.

I love her.

Agnes stirs her oatmeal, waiting for it to cool before taking a bite. "Gus is a romantic. Sends me poetry from the greats and writes his own, too. He runs a business that specifically caters to children. I don't know who could possibly be mad at a man like that."

I shake my head. "I have only theories, but no obvious leads."

"Bill?" she offers, a wry look to her. "I certainly

wouldn't be too surprised if it turned out to be Bill who lost his temper and took a swing at poor Gus."

I shake my head. "I know that's the consensus, but I don't think it's Bill. He's mean, but not violent. I don't think anyone could get that worked up over soup." But as I say it, I know that's not entirely true. Bill gets worked up about things all the time with no rhyme or reason. He doesn't exactly have the steadiest barometer for handling frustrations—mild or major.

Still, I refuse to believe it could be Bill.

Agnes sips her water. "Then who else could it be?"

I hesitate to offer up my guess. "I mean, I don't think Laura Miller would hurt Gus. I really don't. But she's been kicked out of the Soup Alleyoop because her kids were getting too wild a few times. Her son told me that she followed Gus into the kitchen and started yelling at him." I shake my head. "I feel bad even thinking it might be her, which it's not. It can't be. She's a mother."

Agnes quirks an eyebrow at me. "Have you met those children? I might be capable of murder if I had to wrangle them for even a few hours."

I chuckle because she is not far off. "Marianne and Carlos had to come help me out when I offered to babysit for Laura and Dennis. I'm a little out of practice with babysitting, and I think they smelled an easy kill."

Agnes throws her head back. "Tell me you didn't. Oh, Charlotte. And then you came over to take care of me?"

"Not on the same day. And you didn't need taking care of. You just needed a little push."

Agnes, softens. "I don't know who could have hurt Gus. When I go over there today, I'll ask him if he has any theories." She smirks at me. "Once he picks his jaw up off the floor at the sight of me."

"That's my girl."

After I finish my orange juice, I set to making sandwiches for Agnes and Gus to enjoy for lunch. I cut up fruit and pack a few extra items I think they might like.

Really, Gus will be focused on the woman of his dreams returning his affections in more than just handwritten letters. He won't care about the sandwiches.

I love the romance of their connection, and the patience Gus has had while waiting for Agnes to soften her heart again. Now that she is ready, I can't wait for her to finally take that leap into his open arms.

13

SAVORY SOUPS

*A*fter I send Agnes with well-wishes as she prepares to face her butterflies head on, I spend the early morning hours baking my heart out. I am shocked that I have not fallen behind on anything except for selecting a Flavor of the Month cupcake, which I promise myself I will put some real thought into... someday soon.

I drive home so I can shower and get dressed for my unofficial second job, wherein I transform from cupcake baker to soup maker.

Like a true superhero.

Per Gus' written instructions, his recipes are not to be left out, but are to be locked in a safe that only Hunter and myself have the key to.

I open the safe and start gathering the ingredients for the Manhattan clam chowder, which I still haven't tasted. I put three pots of soup on the burners atop the stove, coaxing the fire to life so the soups I made yesterday begin to marry their flavors together and create an aroma in the kitchen that cannot be resisted by the repeat customers.

I don't need to taste the soup; my nose is the barometer I rely on even more than my tastebuds. If it smells like I might want to slurp it down—even though it has slug-like chewie clams in it—then I'm on the right track.

I see no need to confront my culinary bias against clams, oysters, and the like anytime soon.

If the recipes were more straightforward, I would have them memorized by now, but as there are many steps and specific ways Gus wants each ingredient treated, I go line by line.

When Hunter comes in ten minutes after I arrive, he inhales with a grateful smile. "You know, I honestly can't tell the difference between your soup and Gus'. That's a high compliment. It took me half a year to get it right."

"Well, it's not my soup. It's all Gus' recipe. But thank you. I'm glad to know he can step away when he needs to, and the place doesn't fall apart."

Hunter high-fives me because we actually do make quite the team.

The phone rings through the kitchen, which normally is my job to answer while Hunter is on the floor. But as I have a wooden spoon in my hands and everything I touch ends up stinking like onions, Hunter does me a solid and picks up the phone for me.

"Soup Alleyoop. How can I help you?" But his chipper greeting fades with the person's response.

I try to make myself invisible, but the carrots are particularly loud this morning. Each chop that resounds through the kitchen is something I feel like I should apologize for.

"Look, Gus has been more than patient, turning you away time and time again. When the answer's no, the answer's no. He will call you if he changes his mind. No respectable person caves just because they are pestered to death. Calling the restaurant is something Gus and I have asked you to stop doing." He pauses for the person's response. Hunter scoffs, his upper lip curling. "Me? You think *I'd* give you the recipes? You're disgusting. Maybe instead of spending all this time obsessing over getting your hands on his recipe, you could be spending your mornings in the kitchen, creating something worth consuming."

Then Hunter bangs the phone on the hook, causing me to startle.

Not the best thing when I've got a knife in my hand.

"That sounded intense." I try to pry without being completely obvious that that's what I'm doing. I'm eager to know who keeps calling Gus, wanting his recipe. If they would call over and over for it, would they cause bodily harm for it?

Hunter frowns at the phone. "It's just Clancy. Again. And again. Honestly, I don't know why he thinks Gus will consider an offer from him after refusing to negotiate this many times. Unbelievable."

"Clancy wants Gus' soup recipe?"

Hunter's head bobs. "Yup. Wants it. Wants to pay a high premium for it, too. Gus could retire on what Clancy is willing to pay to get his hands on the recipe." He jerks his thumb toward the phone. "Gus asked him to stop calling the restaurant, but that was him trying to get me on the phone to see if I would sell my boss out and hand over the recipes." He shakes his head, clearly disgusted. "Unbelievable."

My brows shoot upward. "I didn't realize the soup industry was so competitive."

Hunter shrugs, looping his whistle over his tall head of blond hair. "We all have our obsessions, I guess. I mean, take basketball. People make careers on being able to put a ball through a hoop. Making and selling the best soup in the country I'm guessing isn't all that strange a quest." He hops up to plop his backside on the counter, sitting on his fingers while he watches me cook. "Clancy is the vice president of Savory Soups."

My mouth pops open in awe. "The stuff they sell in a can at the grocery store? *That* Savory Soups?"

Hunter nods. "One and the same. You know your product is good if established, household name businesses call at least once a week to get their hands on your recipe." He rolls his head from one side to the other, stretching his neck until I hear something pop. "Gus doesn't want his product mass-produced and shoved into cans. He's an artist." Hunter shrugs at his odd phrasing when I smile. "He just uses vegetables and whatnot to make something amazing, while the more predictable artists use paints and clay to do their thing."

I soften my need to get to the bottom of the mystery when Hunter's words sizzle in my chest. "I love that. I want to be that kind of person. Someone who views their work as art." My mouth pulls to the side. "I think sometimes I do that, but other times, I'm punching the clock."

Hunter swings his legs to heft himself off the counter after he glances at the clock on the wall. "Only you can fix that. The good news is, it's fixable, Charlie-girl."

I purse my lips as I go back to chopping carrots. Instead of delving further into the muck of Gus' attack, I let my mind drift to cupcakes.

February is taken over largely by Valentine's Day. Aunt Winnie mentioned last night that the decorations will start going up today throughout Sweetwater Falls.

The typical choice is a red velvet cupcake, which is nothing to sneeze at. But it also doesn't wow me. I've done it before. Everyone's done it before, especially on Valentine's Day.

But Gus makes Manhattan clam chowder, which isn't exactly anything new. In fact, it's usually not even anyone's favorite variety of clam chowder. But he decided to be a soup artist, and put his own hard work, integrity, and heart into the pot.

And now he's being chased down by execs who need his soup recipe.

I want that. Not the being chased part, but the bit about putting my heart and soul into a classic just because I love what I do.

I can make art out of any old cupcake.

The challenge rises in my chest, and before I know it, I'm daydreaming in cupcakes while I chop the rest of the carrots.

I can do this. I can take a classic and infuse it with my love.

After all, if I've learned anything from Gus, that's what artists do.

14

GUS THE ARTIST

I don't know Gus. I mean, if I've met him, I can't recall it. I also can't recall shaking his hand or anything that might put his visage in my mind.

But after I finish making my cupcake flavor of the month, there is only one person on my list whose opinion matters to me before I can declare it good.

Getting his address from Agnes was the easy part. Ringing the doorbell is the part that is proving problematic. Gus is a real artist—one who studies and perfects and stands by his product. His recipes are complicated because he cares.

It takes me three deep inhales, but finally, I ring the doorbell. I hold my breath the entire time it takes for him to mosey to the front door and open it, his brows pleasantly wrinkled at my impromptu presence. "Oh, hello. Was I expecting you? Are you from the hospital?"

Gus can't be more than five-and-a-half feet tall. He's got a ring of white hair around his temples, brown eyes with a soft kindness to them, and strong forearms I can see clearly because the cuffs on his green dress shirt are rolled.

I'm nervous. It's as if I'm meeting someone famous whom I should not be bothering with my normal-person antics. I cannot deign to picture myself in the same room as his genius, yet here I am, on his porch. "Hello, Sir. I'm Charlotte McKay, Winifred's niece."

Recognition dawns on him. "Yes! Oh, hello Charlotte. Yes, it's good to meet you face to face. I'm so grateful for you. Hunter hasn't stopped singing your praises."

I smile, my shoulders relaxing at his jovial demeanor. Though he is thin and his skin is sagging, his chocolate-colored eyes are full of life. He is well into his seventies and seems to be winded from the short trip to opening the door.

"The appreciation is mutual. Hunter is awesome. I'm sorry to stop by unannounced. I had a..." Now I feel silly.

I'm here to give you a cupcake?

I'm here to see if a sweet old man will lie to me and call my cupcake art?

Why do I need Gus' opinion? He is a perfect stranger to me.

But after making his recipes, I feel connected to him even though this is the first time we have formally met.

I clear my throat and try to conjure up enough courage to speak my truth.

I am Charlotte the Brave. Or, I'm supposed to be, at least.

"I respect you," I start out, which is probably the most awkward way to greet a stranger. I shake my head and start over. "I see how much care goes into your soup. I wanted to tell you that I respect you. I thought we should meet, since I'm cooking in your kitchen. I wanted to assure you that the recipes stay in the locked safe, and I follow everything you wrote down to the letter."

Gus regards me with surprise and mild appreciation. "Oh, well, thank you, Charlotte. That's good to know. Honestly, I was in such bad shape for a while that I didn't have the space to do a proper interview. I had to go with my gut. When Agnes vouched for your integrity, I didn't question it."

I heave a sigh of relief. "Thank you." Then the real reason for my visit bubbles in my esophagus, begging me to give voice to my angst. "That's not the only reason I'm here." I hold up the small pink box. "I actually make cupcakes."

Gus nods, and then waves me in. "I'm not supposed to be standing for all that long. Come on in. I've got a pot of coffee brewing that I'm not supposed to finish all by myself. You might have to save me from my bad habits."

I follow him into the home that is neat and very much dated. Everything looks like it was bought in the seventies, complete with yellowed carpet and a brown flower pattern on his couch.

He walks slowly through the living room to his kitchen and motions to the spare wooden chair for me to sit with him. He pours two cups of coffee, and like an old man should, he drinks it black and doesn't offer sugar or milk.

It's pretty much a punishment, drinking coffee this way, but I don't complain aloud.

Gus takes a sip and smacks his lips before he sets down his mug. "I think I know why you're here. You want me to put your cupcakes on the menu." He shakes his head kindly but firmly to cut off my reply. "I'm sorry, Charlotte. I'm sure they're tasty, but I'm not in the habit of changing my menu. I sell soup, and that's that."

I press my lips together before I respond. "I'm not actually here for that. I assumed as much, looking at your menu. I'm here because... because I respect you as an artist. I see how much love goes into your soups, how fiercely you protect the vision of your restaurant. I want to be like that with my business. I own the Bravery Bakery. I sell only cupcakes, just like you sell only soup."

Gus nods. "Agnes mentioned. I've heard great things about it, but I'm afraid I've never had much of a sweet tooth."

"I'm here because I want you to try my cupcake. I don't know why I need you to be the one to test my flavor of the month, but it has to be you. Red velvet doesn't excite me, but I decided to try to put my spin on the classic, like you did with your soups. You don't have crazy kinds of soup;

you have varieties people are familiar with, but you put your own spin on them. That's what I tried to do here, but I don't know if I nailed it." I shake my head as I pop open the box to show him my creation. "I don't need someone with a sweet tooth. I need an artist."

Emotion shimmers in Gus' glassy eyes. His hand moves to his heart, where I can see his fat knuckles that know their way around the kitchen. "Young lady, that is the most beautiful compliment I have ever been paid. Sure, I'll try your cupcake. I'd be honored."

My chin drops with relief as I push the box toward him. I feel the need to compensate for the cupcake's perceived shortcomings before he has even tasted a bite. "The cream cheese frosting isn't sharp enough. The red velvet cake is good, but it's what you might expect. Is it enough of a reinvention?"

I chew on my nail as he takes the cake out of the box, examining it from all angles. "It's a cute little thing," he remarks.

My head bobs. "I'm more worried about the flavor."

"Ah, but people eat with their eyes first. If this is a Valentine's Day dessert, perhaps consider making it big enough for two. Couples can share it, and people who are alone on Valentine's Day get double the cake to enjoy. Everybody wins."

My eyes brighten. "You're giving me notes!" I exclaim, my spine straightening.

124 | MOLLY MAPLE

"I assume that's what you came here for. Anyone can make a dessert sweet. Anyone can make a soup that warms you up. But artists like us?" He leans toward me, his voice dripping with passion. "We want an experience. We want joy in a bowl—or in a cupcake wrapper. Think about the kind of day your client has had when they are about to order this. Think about *why* they need it. What would drive them to connect with this particular cupcake when you've got other flavors to offer?"

I nod eagerly. "Thank you! Yes. Keep the advice coming. This is gold."

Gus chuckles, inhaling the cupcake. "Mm. That smells nice. Not too sugary." He studies the cupcake from all angles after peeling off the wrapping. "No one's favorite flavor of soup is chicken noodle, but they order it again and again because it's a classic that makes them feel cared for. Their mom or dad might have opened a can for them when they came down with a cold when they were little. I want that experience for them. I want them to remember what it is to be cared for." He holds the cupcake aloft. "A red velvet cupcake is nice, but it's like chicken noodle soup. It's no one's favorite, but they'll order it because it's the cupcake they know. Also, when paired with a romantic holiday, it's the dessert they'll want to complete the ritual of red-painted romance."

I swoon at his beautiful language. I can see why Agnes has been so taken with his love letters to her. If he writes even half as poetically as he talks, I don't know how Agnes stayed away for whole years.

Give me poetry about cupcakes, and I'm a goner.

When Gus opens his mouth to take a bite after peeling back the wrapper, I nearly leap off the table to stop him. "Wait!"

Gus startles, staring at me as if I have gone insane. "Is something wrong?"

"Everything is wrong! I have to fix this cupcake before you try it. I know what's wrong. What's missing. Don't try that. It's a stupid red velvet cupcake. It's not an experience, but I can fix that."

Gus chuckles at my enthusiasm as he puts it down on the table. "I can wait for perfection. It's often the only thing worth waiting for. You say you can make this even better? I want to see it first thing. Before the public, I want to see the art unveiled, if I'm not being too presumptuous."

I nod, standing to leave because I don't want to lose this spark Gus has created in me. "Absolutely. I have to go. I need to fix the cupcake tonight, or I won't be able to sleep."

Gus laughs at my sincerity. "I can respect that. Thank you, Charlotte. It was a joy to not share a cupcake with you."

I salute him, grabbing up my purse. "The restaurant is in good hands, Gus. Hunter loves you and keeps things running smoothly. When Clancy called to try to get your recipe, he didn't miss a beat."

Gus' smile fades, but he doesn't scowl. He more looks

sad that he can't share his recipe, but wishes he could find a nice way to do so, where everyone wins. "Clancy is a determined one, I'll give him that. I would expect no less from a Navy man, like myself."

"You were in the Navy? Did you know Clancy back then?"

Gus shakes his head with a wistful smile. "No. But I understand his grit." He runs his hand over his face. "Clancy tried to use our shared service background to bond with me so I would give him my recipes."

I stand near the exit but pause before leaving. "What I don't understand is how anyone could have hurt you. I'm so sorry that happened."

Gus lowers his chin sadly. "I thought for sure it was Bill. He's always so determined to get me to sell his broccoli cheese soup at my restaurant, but I don't think it's a good fit."

I scoff at Gus' restraint. "That's a nice way of putting it. Bill's soup is terrible."

Gus chortles at my blunt assessment. "Which makes it not a good fit for my place. But the police say Bill had an alibi, so it wasn't him who attacked me. I feel bad for suspecting him in the first place. I can't imagine who would knock me out and tie me up. I wish I'd seen any of it so I could point the police in the right direction. The sheriff is probably frustrated with me, since I have no useful information to give."

I cannot imagine anyone would be frustrated with Gus,

sweet as he is. "It's going to be okay, Gus. They'll get to the bottom of this soon enough."

I walk out of Gus' home with a clear direction of where I am headed. I will solve this cupcake conundrum.

And then I am going to solve the crime against Gus.

15

BIRTHDAY PARTY ENTERTAINMENT

I am buzzing this morning, and it's not just because I'm on a sugar overload. I chop the potatoes with gusto. I dance around the kitchen with the knife in my hand as I search for more onions. I feel light, like it matters that I'm happy, and my happiness makes the world around me better.

Hunter laughs when he comes into the kitchen, sweating with his whistle in his hand. "Tell me you've been dancing like this while I've been out there, pulling kids off the hoop. It gives me hope that something happy is going on in here while I'm trying not to lose it."

"Rough crowd?"

"The roughest. We've got a birthday party out there. The one-week ban on the Miller children is up, so the birthday boy is in full-on overload."

I brighten. "Oh! I didn't realize Nathan, Marvin and

Benji were out there. I'll go say hello in a minute." I frown at the big bag of onions that is hanging beside the fridge. "Can you help me with this? I usually cut open the bag, but I need just one onion, so I don't want to cut the whole thing down."

Hunter trots to the fridge area. "Oh, yeah. You're going to have to cut it down. Gus' knots are insane. He was in the Navy, you know. Give me a second; I'll cut it for you." He looks over his shoulder at me while he gets to work sawing the thick knots with a steak knife. "I can't wait until Gus comes back. He was given the all clear this morning. I imagine he'll be in tomorrow, which means you're off the hook."

My knife droops in my hand, and my potato chopping comes to a halt. "Oh. I guess that's a good thing. I mean, burning the candle at both ends hasn't been all that great." A whine comes out of my mouth before I can stop it. "But I like it here!"

Hunter chuckles at my childishness. "Then you should stay. It's not like Gus is going to turn down a quality employee. He's not getting any younger." It's meant as an offhanded statement, but I can tell by the tensing of Hunter's shoulders that he is sad to see the passing of time affect a soul as pure as Gus. "And you know I like having you around."

I shake my head. "No. It's a temporary thing, me being here. I'll turn in my apron when Gus comes back. But I'm going to be sad about it. I might even pout."

"I've been warned." Hunter gives me a dramatic frown. "I'll be sad, too. It won't be the same around here without you, Charlie-girl." He grunts once at the effort of cutting down the onion bag and then smiles triumphantly. "There! I did it. Gus always tries to teach me his knots, but I'm no expert. It's a Navy thing that apparently only the quality sailors understand."

I hold up a finger after Hunter sets the sack on the counter. "I'll be back in a minute. I want to say hello to the birthday boy." I take off my apron and make my way to the eating area, waving when I see Laura.

In true Miller fashion, the three boys are wild. When pumped with birthday cupcakes from the Bravery Bakery, they are absolutely out of control. I recognize my handiwork smeared across the faces of each child in attendance while the mothers in the area ply themselves with copious amounts of soup.

Laura pauses from her soup to smile at me. "Charlotte! You have no idea how well your cupcakes go with soup. I'm so glad I outsourced the baking to you."

The other parents aren't giving Laura a wide berth today. In fact, they are all chatting animatedly while they eat. Though, upon closer inspection, I see they are around her, but no one is really interacting with her.

I motion to the party. "You've got your hands full. Where is the birthday boy?" I pretend not to see Benji, so he has to get off the nearby table and come to me if he wants to make his presence known. "I don't see him."

The newly minted six-year-old runs to me, jumping in front of me with both hands raised. "Me! I'm the birthday boy! It's my special day! You want a cupcake?"

It's a sweet offering. In fact, no one has offered me a cupcake in quite some time.

I cast him a smile and hop in front of him to match his rhythm. "I'm working, but thank you. Are you enjoying your…" But I don't get to finish my sentence before Benji runs off to chase an errant basketball.

Laura is pretty much checked out, shoveling soup into her mouth because she knows her time here is limited.

I sit in the booth with her and fix her with a kind smile, which is a far cry from the veiled looks of judgment the other parents are giving her. "Hi, Laura. You holding up okay?"

She nods, but I can tell it's a lie. "Why did I throw a birthday party? Remind me why?"

My head tilts to the side. "I can't decide between 'good parent' or 'masochist'."

"Masochist," Laura rules with a dejected chuckle. "At least he's happy. They'll sleep well tonight after all this jumping around."

"Here's hoping. Anything I can do to help?"

"Pray for the sun to set."

I can tell Laura is only half-joking.

I reach across the table and pat her hand. Then I notice a gift that's been unwrapped sitting on the presents table atop a basketball-themed paper table covering. "Benji got a set of baseballs?" I ask.

Laura nods with dread. "I can already picture them going through the neighbor's window."

"Can I borrow them for a minute or two?"

Laura quirks an eyebrow at me. "Be my guest."

I take the three balls out of their package, ignoring the chaos around me, even when a basketball thumps me on the back.

I catch the eye of Laura's oldest child who is in need of some entertainment before he pulls the basketball hoop off the wall. "Hey, Nathan! Want to show the birthday boy your new skill?"

Nathan raises his brows and then lights up, pausing his chaos to trot over to me. "I've been practicing!" he announces with pride.

"I'm not surprised. All the best jugglers practice. You ready?" I do my best to gather up the rowdy children so Nathan is the center of attention.

Yes, other parents. You can do something to help rein in the chaos, or you can sit there judging Laura.

Everyone is about to get a show they'll remember, more than the rowdiness of the children.

Nathan starts with two balls, much to the amusement of the others. Then after a few beats, I help him incorporate the third, much to the amazement of the adults.

It truly is incredible to watch this preteen boy go from ruffian to completely focused and controlled. Even Laura begins clapping in a slow rhythm to cheer him on. Every adult's mouth is dropped open, and several soup spoons are frozen halfway to their destination. The entire dining area becomes transfixed by the impromptu show.

Nathan juggles without dropping anything for several minutes, which has to be some sort of record. When he finishes, the only sound is laughter and clapping. There are no sighs from tired parents, no crying children, and no one is trying to tear apart the place in the name of good fun.

Everyone is just... happy.

I love it. I love the look of pride on Nathan's face as he bows like a seasoned professional, especially when paired with the adoration beaming from his mother.

I didn't realize Hunter was by my side, but suddenly, I hear his voice to my left. "How did you do that?"

"I didn't do anything," I admit. "That was all Nathan."

"I mean, how did you get everyone to calm down?"

I shrug and point to the Miller family, who is all smiles and glee. It's a beautiful picture, and one I am glad I got to be there to witness.

I'm going to miss working here at the Soup Alleyoop.

16

BILL'S BETTER BEHAVIOR

*B*ill's Diner is loud. The dining area is filled to the brim with every table taken and a line at the stand.

It's just as well. I'm not here to eat.

I'm here on a mission, so I don't stop at the hostess stand, but wave to Becca, the waitress I trained to replace me back when I worked here. I march into the kitchen with my confrontation face firmly in place.

"Bill," I say loudly, as if I am announcing some scandal.

My former boss drops his ladle and wipes his hands on his stained apron. His thick brows push together. "If you need a job, you can start by scrubbing down the tables out there."

I narrow my eyes at him. "We've been over this. I have a job. I have a business, just like you. I'm not here to work. I'm here to teach an old dog some new tricks."

Bill snorts at me while the cook throws butter on the griddle. "How's that?"

I motion to myself. "I know that I am the only person in this town who finds your surly attitude endearing, which is why I'm here, telling you to your face that you need to apologize to Gus."

I don't even need to summon my Charlotte the Brave persona. I'm naturally worked up enough to put a bow on this loose end so no one else trips over it ever again.

Bill laughs bitterly that this is why I stormed into his kitchen. "I don't think you know me all that well, Charlotte McKay."

I stare him down, arms akimbo. "I don't think you know me at all if you think I'm going to sit back and let you get accused of beating up an old man."

Bill's laughter dies on his tongue. He looks almost comical as he tilts his head at me. "Wait, what?"

I don't soften an inch but hold my ground. "That's right. You know you're on the suspect list in Gus' case. You and I both know that you didn't attack sweet old Gus. Don't be a jerk. Go choke on your pride and call up Gus right this minute. Apologize for being a pest." I hold up my hand when Bill starts to protest. "Yes, you were a pest. You were such a pest and so unpleasant that people assumed you would go so far as to hit an old man over the head. You're going to apologize."

Bill's lower lip juts out like the overgrown child he often is. "I'll do no such thing."

I am just unhinged enough from baking all morning and then making soup and refereeing wild children all afternoon and evening that I have no ability to hold back. I go for Bill's weak spot, and because I know him, I know exactly what that is.

I snatch two potholders off the hook and stomp to the pot of broccoli cheese soup.

Ack. Even simmering in the pot, it smells wretched.

"What are you doing?" Bill calls after me, but I can't be bothered to slow down to accommodate his defective conscience.

I tilt the pot precariously over the sink. "Take out your phone and call Gus right this instant. Even if he now knows you didn't attack him, you were so mean to him that he thought it had to be you. Call Gus and apologize right now, or you can say goodbye to your precious broccoli cheese soup."

Bill's eyes widen as he cries out. It's as if I have his newborn child dangling over a balcony, the way he is reacting. "No! No, don't do it!"

"Make that call, Bill! Nice and loud so I can hear you making Gus your new best friend. Now!"

Bill keeps his panicked gaze fixed on me while he fumbles with his phone. "I'm calling! I'm calling!"

"Best be quick with that apology, Bill. I don't know how long I can hold this pot without my fingers slipping!"

"No!" Bill has one hand in his hair and the other clutching the phone as if he is in the middle of a hostage negotiation. When the call connects, he rushes to make things right. "Gus, it's Bill. I shouldn't have pushed you so hard to try to get you to serve my soup at your restaurant."

Good start, but I want an actual apology, and Bill knows it.

I tip the pot, watching as a small slosh spills out into the sink.

"Oops," I lie, as if it was an accident.

Bill's voice climbs with borderline hysteria. "It was too much, and I'm sorry. You know how to run your business. How can I make it up to you?"

I nod but don't put the pot down. *Good. That's good,* I mouth to Bill, encouraging him to keep up the decent behavior for as long as it will last.

Whatever Gus is saying, I'm sure Bill isn't hearing. He responds with a rushed, "Come by the diner tomorrow, and I'll fix you a meal on the house. A little apology burger to set things right."

When I place the pot on the stainless-steel counter, Bill's anxiety fades in waves. He puts his hand over his heart, as if he is nearing a cardiac event at the threat of his soup being messed with.

Bill's shoulders lower as he breathes in deep. "Gus, whoever put you in the hospital is on my list, alright? We should stick together, instead of butting heads. When I find out who did this, they're never stepping foot in my diner ever again."

I nod, appreciating that last bit, as it came from Bill under no duress of his soup being thrown down the sink.

When Bill ends the call, he lowers his chin but still aims a glower my way. "Are you happy now?"

"Thrilled." I slap my hands in satisfaction. "I think my work here is done. But I've gotta say, if you make me come back here because you're so mean you get yourself into trouble like this again, I'm not hesitating. That whole pot is going down the drain. You got me?"

Bill holds up his hands in surrender. "Fine, fine. You know, Gus could have compromised a little."

My nostrils flare as my hand secures to the pot's handle. "Bill, don't test me on this!"

Bill takes a panicked step forward. "I take it back! I pushed Gus too hard. No means no, and all that. I won't do that again. I'll make nice when he comes in tomorrow for a burger. I won't even serve him a cup of my soup, unless he asks for it."

"That's what I like to hear." I point my finger at him before I make my way to the exit. "Underneath that scowl, you're one of my favorite people in this town. Don't make me this mad ever again."

Bill lowers his chin. "Okay, okay."

I march out of the diner into the glow of the fading sunlight flickering off the snow.

I might not be able to fix all of Gus' problems, but I think I might have helped with at least one.

TRESPASSER TROUBLE

*a*gnes is a new woman. Not only has she lost the cloud that's accumulated over her head as of late, but she now travels with a constant smile. I hung out with her last night, and she was a brand-new glowing angel. I went over to her house after I confronted Bill. I needed her help with a needlepoint project. The entire time I was there, she was singing to herself while we crafted together.

I love it. It does my heart good to see happiness on the people I love.

It's been a long stint of working two jobs, but I've managed well enough. I am only a little behind at the Bravery Bakery, but it's nothing I can't catch up on, since last night was my final day making soup.

I wake up with a crick in my neck, but the bigger unhappiness is that I forgot to turn in my apron when I closed down the restaurant last night. Instead of leaving it on the hook, I accidentally wore it all the way until I parked at Bill's Diner, and then realized my mistake.

I guess working two jobs might have hit its breaking point.

At least I didn't mess up any soups or cupcakes.

Well, if I'm being honest, my first attempt at the red velvet cupcake was a flop. I mean, sure, it was a cupcake, but it was nothing special.

I don't want to sell something that isn't special. Anyone can do that. I want to do something no one else can do. I want my cupcakes to infuse my client with joy and nostalgia.

I want to be worth the gamble.

As I brush my teeth and get dressed for the day, I know I have two stops to make before I head over to the Bravery Bakery to start up the several dozen batches of the cupcake flavor of the month. When I checked the website this morning, I had fourteen dozen orders of just that flavor, plus a plethora of my other varieties.

I tug my messy blonde curls into a ponytail and scamper down the steps, kissing Aunt Winnie on the cheek before I shove my feet into winter boots and head out the door into the frosty February morning air.

This is going to be a good day. I can feel it.

I bake my heart out, which is the only way to exist in a kitchen, in my opinion. Throwing the ingredients together is never a drudgery, but a dance only I get to perform.

I nuzzle my nose to the fishbowl, singing to Buttercream while she flicks her tail at me happily. My goldfish doesn't mind if I sing off-key, or if my dance moves aren't exactly cutting edge. Logan won her for me at the Twinkle Lights Festival, back when I could not fathom someone so wonderful could ever be interested in me.

My, how far I've come. Months ago, I moved to Sweetwater Falls with barely any money, my big city ego bruised, and my tail between my legs. Now I have a best friend, a sweet boyfriend and a cupcake shop all my own.

Each of those things required bravery, and every one of those actions were totally worth the risk of stepping out of my comfort zone, which, as it turned out, wasn't comfortable at all.

It was safe, and that was the only upside.

As my cupcakes bake and my frostings come together, my heart swells with gratitude for this small town, and all the life lessons it has given me thus far.

I know I have nailed the flavor of the month, but there is one opinion that matters to me more than most for this particular challenge. Though he doesn't have a sweet tooth, I need Gus' stamp of approval on this cupcake before the sun sets tonight.

I throw my apron from the restaurant over my shoulder and pack up two cupcakes: one for Gus and one for Hunter, for being so easy to work with. Today is the first day Gus will be back on his feet at the Soup Alleyoop.

I daresay he should start his day with one of the best cupcakes in the world.

I drive to the restaurant with a smile on my face, because once again, I have grown. I didn't back down from the challenge to create something I love. I didn't fall back and attempt something easy simply because I can lower the bar for myself whenever life gets the tiniest bit complicated. Gus' standard of perfection pushed me to raise the bar for myself.

That's how I know this cupcake is good.

I can't wait to see his face when he tries it.

But when I enter the Soup Alleyoop half an hour before opening time, Hunter's voice hits my ears with anger I am unfamiliar hearing on him. Even when the kids are insane and breaking things, he doesn't sound mad, only loud enough to get the place back in order.

I wince at the vitriol in Hunter's voice. "You had better have a good explanation as to why you're here."

Another man's voice replies. "I was just stopping by to talk to Gus to see if we could come to an agreement, is all."

I stand near the entrance without taking another step forward. I want to know what I am walking into before I make my next move.

Hunter is livid. I can hear it even through the wall that separates the kitchen from the main area of the restaurant. "Give me one good reason why I shouldn't call the police. I know for a fact those doors were locked. You're breaking and entering, and I'm not having it."

Hunter might be willing to wait for an explanation, but I am not. I tug out my phone and keep near the front door, out of sight while I call Logan.

The fact that my boyfriend is a police officer comes in handy on occasions like this.

I set down my purse, the cupcakes and the apron, speaking quietly into my phone when Logan picks up. "Hey, someone broke into the Soup Alleyoop. Can you come with backup?"

Logan asks me a few questions, wanting details I just don't have. I don't know who is in the kitchen with Hunter, or how long they've been here. I don't know if there's been any damage, only that there is a man in the Soup Alleyoop who does not belong here and should not have access to the restaurant before it has opened for the day.

With Logan on the way, I debate hanging back and waiting for the police to show up and do their thing.

But when Hunter's voice goes from livid to a gasp of horror, my feet find themselves moving toward the kitchen, whether it's a good idea or not. If I can handle being Hunter's backup in the middle of a Miller boy's birthday party, then I can handle helping him out through whatever is going on in the kitchen.

Or I can find myself in deep trouble.

Either way, I'm not about to stand out here when Hunter might be in danger. He's a good person, and Gus needs good people with him while he runs the business of his dreams.

I gather my gumption and march as quietly as I can into the kitchen, unprepared for the scene that greets me. Before I can stop myself, I shout out, "Hunter, no!"

18

THE CLASH OF THE SOUPS

I don't know the man with whom Hunter is struggling. All I know is that he is at least fifty, and is currently grunting with frustration in Hunter's capable grip.

"Call the cops, Charlie!" Hunter shouts to me, his face red from the fight. He has the man in a bear hug from behind, securing him in place while the older man gasps and splutters.

"What are you doing?" I yell at him.

Hunter never loses his temper with the rowdy children. He has a fondness for Gus that goes beyond amiable coworkers. My mind is having a hard time reconciling the sight before me with Hunter's usually congenial nature. "You're hurting him!" I protest.

But Hunter shakes his head, his teeth gritted. "He took

a swing at me. Call the police, Charlie. Hurry! It's him! He did it. He hurt Gus!"

The man in Hunter's grip shakes his head, pleading with me to intervene and take his side. "No! I would never! This guy just attacked me out of nowhere! Help!"

I don't know what to do, so I stand there, frozen and unable to offer any help at all, because I have no idea who is telling the truth and who is guilty of hurting Gus.

"He did it!" the man tells me. "He's the one who hit Gus! Hunter tied him up because Gus wouldn't give him the business!"

Hunter's upper lip curls. "Are you kidding me? Gus is like a father to me. I don't care about the business nearly as much as I care about him."

I want to believe Hunter, but the other man's theory is logical enough.

Hunter admitted that he loves it here. He told me that the profits were high and the expenses were low. He knows everything about running this place, including the coveted recipes.

It's not outside the realm of possibility that Hunter might want to take Gus out so he can take over the Soup Alleyoop. I don't want to believe it, but I can't dismiss it, either.

Hunter meets my eyes with an earnest plea for me to truly hear him. "Charlie, it's me. I didn't hurt Gus. This here is Clancy. He's been after Gus' recipes from day one. He was in here when I came in this morning to open."

Clancy's eyes widen with desperation as he struggles against Hunter, who is in the prime of his life. "He lured me here! Said he would give me Gus' recipes, but it was a trap! It was all a trap!" He moans loudly. "Don't tell me you're setting up this young lady, too!"

Hunter jerks Clancy without mercy. "Knock it off. You're done. You hear me? No one ties up Gus and gets away with it."

A clue dings in my head that I should have connected before. "Clancy, were you in the Navy?"

Clancy nods, though he looks just as confused as Hunter as to why I would ask that question right now, in the middle of their battle. "A Navy man would never do something unthinkable like that!" he wails, heaving a gasp when Hunter jerks him to the left.

In that moment, I know exactly what happened.

And I know who attacked poor Gus.

I take out my phone and call Logan once more. "I know who did it."

Logan's reply is rushed. "Charlotte, tell me you're safely outside. Tell me you're not in there."

"I can't tell you that," I answer slowly, watching Hunter struggle against Clancy, who is giving his attempt at escape all he's got. "It was Clancy—the vice president of Savory Soups. He hurt Gus, Logan. You have to hurry."

"Get out of there!" Logan yells.

I end the call, because I know I cannot do what he is asking. I can't leave Hunter alone with a dangerous man.

"You did it," I tell Clancy. "You know how to tie those complicated sailor knots. It was you all along. Hunter doesn't know how to untie sailor's knots, so I can't imagine he would know how to tie them properly. You did it. You're the one who attacked Gus."

No sooner do I work out the truth does Clancy break loose from Hunter's grip. He turns and punches Hunter across the face, and then barrels straight toward me.

I should have trusted Hunter.

I should have run out of the building when Logan told me to go. Now that the truth has come to light, Clancy's wild eyes focus on me.

19

CLANCY'S CRUELTY

I cry out in pain when Clancy slams me into the side of the stainless-steel countertop. "Stop!"

Clancy's hands go around my throat, as if that will undo the truth I just let loose into the air. "You don't know what you're talking about, girl!"

Hunter holds the side of his face where Clancy just punched him, looking equal parts stunned and wounded. He reaches out his free hand and shouts at the aggressor. "Let her go!"

I fight against Clancy's grip as best I can, clawing at his meaty hands to get them off me, but his fury is the edge he needs to keep me in place. He doesn't want the truth to come out, because that will be the end of him and his career.

My passion is cupcakes, and they matter a great deal to me. But I cannot imagine caring so much that I would choke someone for it. That I would hit an old man on the head. That I would tie someone up and shove them in a closet.

I struggle against Clancy, his grizzled breath heating my face while I fight for the right to breathe.

"I was good to Gus. That deal was fair and the best he could ever hope to have. I wasn't going to do anything but produce his soup in our factory. I even offered to put his name somewhere on the soup's label! No matter what I offered, he wouldn't budge."

My eyes bug while my knees begin to lose their ability to hold me upright. My vision swims while I claw and rip whatever I can reach on Clancy's body.

"Twenty years in this business! Twenty years, and we've never tried a product as good as his. That offer was a high compliment, but he acts like it's not worth his time to even consider it. Gus should have listened to me. For months, I've been trying to reason with him. What's the punishment for being driven past a person's limit? Because I think a bump on the head is the least he should get for all he's put me through!"

My mouth falls open as I fight for air.

"I put my reputation on the line for this deal! I increased what we were going to give him. The president of the company didn't want to go a penny over the initial offer, but I negotiated more for Gus because I know a good product when I taste it. Then he won't take the offer? He won't sign a thing? There is no price that can tempt him?"

Clancy gets in my face, his eyes beady and wild. "He's insane!" Clancy's upper lip curls. "And he's useless now that you're here. Tell me where he keeps the recipes, and I'll let you go!"

My legs are limp and my attempts to escape Clancy's strong grip are a futile waste of the last vestiges of oxygen in my lungs.

I want to fight back, but I can only do so much. I didn't want to believe it was Hunter at fault, but I hesitated, and now I am inches away from death.

All over a soup I've never even tried.

When a loud bang resounds like a gong throughout the kitchen, I get my first gulp of air. My fight is weak, but I manage to shove Clancy's grip off my throat before my legs go out from under me.

My body collapses on the floor in a pile of limbs, and soon after, the weight of a full-grown man in his fifties tumbles down atop me, squishing a puff of air from my lungs.

Hunter stands over us, his chest heaving and a frying pan in his hand. He hits Clancy over the head a second time, and I hear the same gong sound echo through the kitchen, setting my teeth on edge.

"Hold on, Charlie-girl. I'll get him off you," Hunter promises. He takes his sweet time rolling Clancy off my body, and then sits on the floor with me, frying pan still in hand.

Finally, I can breathe. As I lay on the floor of the

kitchen, I wonder what steps I took that led me to this place in my life, where grown men attack me, and the job that was supposed to be temporary ended up being something that I would fight to the death to defend.

Hunter slinks to the floor beside me, leaning his back on the cupboards while he catches breath, his eyes wide. He doesn't help me to sit up, because I'm not sure it's worth the effort at this point. Clancy is out, and it doesn't look like he'll be ready for round two anytime soon.

Clancy sneaked up on Gus because Gus wouldn't sign the contract that would give Savory Soups the recipe to his coveted Manhattan clam chowder soup. All this bitterness over something so simple.

I don't understand greed like that.

I guess it's a good thing Clancy's mania makes no sense to me.

I'm grateful for the air that flows in and out of my lungs. I'm grateful I wasn't alone in this when the epiphany came to me.

Most of all, I'm grateful Gus wasn't here to get hurt all over again. He's a sweet man, and doesn't deserve to have to defend himself against a person whose priorities have clearly gone awry.

"You breathing, Charlie-girl?" Hunter asks me quietly, the frying pan still in his hand. He keeps his eyes on Clancy, waiting for him to stir.

"I think so," I tell Hunter. "You saved my life." My voice

comes out in a croak as I stare up at the ceiling. "Thank you."

Hunter leans his head back, finally exhaling a gust of his nerves. "You trusted me. Thank *you*."

Seconds after I hear the peppering of footsteps coming from the dining area, the sound of Logan's voice bathes me in pure beauty. "Charlotte? Charlotte!"

Above the din, I hear Gus' broken heart as he rushes to Hunter. "No! Hunter, what happened? My poor boy. Are you alright?"

Neither of us are alright, but when arms go around us that will only heal and never harm, I think we are well on our way to never having a dark day like this one ever again.

BRAVING RED VELVET

*I*f I liked Gus before, I find that I adore him now. He tends to Hunter as if the twenty-three-year-old man is a small boy. There is washcloth filled with ice in his wrinkled hand that is pressed to Hunter's cheek, and the most compassionate woebegone look creasing Gus' bushy salt-and-pepper brows. "Tell me everything. Start to finish."

Hunter stands with his back to the counter. He lets Gus baby him because I think we both need a little sweetness after such a salty encounter.

Logan is on the job, but he doesn't leave my side. His partner does the poking around and arresting of the bad guy. Logan keeps checking my throat, which I know can't look great.

Hunter keeps his voice quiet, but Logan and I can hear him just fine. "When I came in to start my shift, the door was open. Not just unlocked, but open. I should have called the police then, but I thought maybe Charlie might have accidentally forgotten to lock up last night, and I didn't want to upset her about the mistake."

"Charlie?" Logan questions.

"Yeah. You know, the Soup Queen."

I snort at the label I did not see coming. "I'm merely the soup helper. I didn't invent the recipes." I offer a courteous tilt of my head to Gus. "Long live the Soup King."

"Fine. Charlie the Soup Helper, it is. Never seen someone throw away a crown so quick." Hunter gives me a weak smile, and then turns back to Gus. "I heard rummaging in the kitchen, so I went back, thinking Charlie decided she was going to come back for one more day, or maybe that you'd beat me to work because you were eager to return."

Gus' eyes sparkle with moisture at the sight of Hunter's cheek bruising in real time. "I was eager to come back here. I'm no good at home with nothing to do all day. If I ever talk of retiring, remind me of how miserable I was for the time I was stuck at the hospital or at home."

"Will do," Hunter assures him. "I came back here and saw Clancy rifling through your desk. He didn't find the safe in the bottom drawer, but if I didn't come in and stop him, I know that's what he was going for."

Logan's arm coils around my hips as he pulls me in for a hug. "So, this is a robbery that you two stopped?"

Hunter holds his hand parallel to the floor and tilts it

from side to side. "I mean, sort of. But Clancy wasn't after the money."

Logan's hug is gentle and firm at the same time. I know I can trust his strength to hold me upright while I exhale at finally being given a safe place.

How I need a safe place after almost being choked to death.

Logan's hand moves over my spine in a soothing circle. "What was he after? Why would he break in, if not to steal money?" Logan glances around. "Is any of your basketball memorabilia valuable?"

Hunter shakes his head, but it's Gus who answers. "Clancy is the vice president of Savory Soups. He's been after me to give him my Manhattan clam chowder recipe for months now." He shakes his head, almost in apology. "But I'm not interested in seeing my creation in a can. I think it might break my heart if I did. The soup is meant to be enjoyed sitting down in a booth while children play in the background."

Hunter picks up where Gus trails off. "Clancy calls at least once a week. Sometimes he stops by, too. Tries to convince Gus to give him the recipe."

Logan's eyebrows lift in amazement. "Wow. Gus, apart from being frightened that your business was broken into, I hope you feel proud that your soup is worth this level of a fight."

Gus grips Logan's shoulder, giving off that grandfatherly vibe that melts my heart. "I am proud. Perhaps too proud, because I couldn't sell the recipe to Clancy, even when the offer got sweeter and sweeter." He lowers his chin. "But maybe if I had sold the recipe, Charlotte and Hunter wouldn't have been attacked today."

Hunter stands straighter, as do I. "No," Hunter rules, and I am right beside him in my protest. "A person who will resort to violence over a deal that didn't happen is the sort to get violent over just about any small slight. You did the right thing, Gus."

I nod vehemently. "Absolutely. Your soup is art. An artist has to be okay with their art being mass-produced. You don't want to see your life's work compromised by a factory. There is a great deal of love that goes into each pot."

At my outburst, Gus finally leaves Hunter's side. Logan releases me only so Gus can hug me while his heart swells. "Young lady, I am so grateful you decided to help us. Love is the key ingredient. When it's missing, the world is less flavorful. I'm so glad you see that."

I don't remember my grandfather. I've seen pictures of me on his lap, but I don't recall anything about his smile, his hugs, or if I did anything to make him laugh.

In this small exchange, I feel my heart attaching to Gus, making him my grandfather, whether we are blood relation or not.

Agnes is sort of like an aunt to me, and she is dating Gus. That's enough of a connection for me to be able to pretend with full confidence that Gus is my family.

We see the world the same way: in shades of possibility and flavors that are yet to be discovered.

Gus kisses my cheek before releasing me.

Then I remember why I came here in the first place. "Oh! I completely forgot. I brought you something."

Gus chuckles. "I was wondering how you got caught up in Clancy's web. Your last day was yesterday."

Logan grimaces. "I'm not doing any actual police work," he admits with palpable chagrin. "I'm supposed to be interviewing you all and taking photos of the crime scene, but when you so much as skin your knee, Miss Charlotte, all my plans fly out the window."

I kiss Logan's cheek. "How about the three of us wait out there in one of the booths. You take your pictures and come get us for questions when you need."

Logan nods. "Thanks. I have a hard time being professional when you're here. I want to be a teenager with his girlfriend, when I need to be the man with a job."

I squeeze his hand and exit the kitchen with Gus and Hunter after I make an ice pack for Hunter's cheek.

The three of us pile into the nearest booth after I grab up my purse, the apron I came here to return, and the small pink box I left on the table near the entrance.

"I reworked the cupcake, Gus," I tell him after I slide into the booth. Then to Hunter, I add, "That's why I came in this morning. I accidentally wore my apron home last night. I was bringing it back this morning for you. I also needed to get Gus' seal of approval on my flavor of the month for the Bravery Bakery."

Gus chortles at my determination that is no less voracious than his when it comes to culinary expertise. "Well, I'm happy to help however I can. If you need me to eat a cupcake, then so be it."

"Thanks for taking one for the team," I joke.

I pop the top open of the pink box and take out what is most certainly the largest cupcake on my menu. It is just over four inches in diameter and stands five inches tall, if you include the perfectly piped frosting.

Gus' eyes widen at the sight as I lift two giant cupcakes from the box.

Hunter claps appreciatively. Hunter eyes his with hunger shining through. "I vote that every time I have to apprehend a burglar, I should get one of these as a reward."

"Deal," I reply without missing a beat. I am overwhelmed with gratitude that Hunter stood up to Clancy.

"Tell me about this work of art," Gus says to me.

"It's a Valentine's Day classic," I start, going with the obvious selling point first. "Red Velvet is the thing people want for their romantic holiday, right? But that flavor has never thrilled me, so I did my own take on it." I motion to the size of the cupcake. "First off, it's meant for two, so you can order a dessert and split it with your special someone. Or, if you are not celebrating Valentine's Day with anyone, then you get the whole dessert for yourself, which is pretty great."

Hunter's eyes widen. "I'm not single. Do I have to share it, or can I eat the whole thing?"

I snicker at his eager nature. "It's all yours."

Hunter grins as much as his swollen cheek will allow. "Thanks, Charlie-girl." He sets down the ice pack beside his giant cupcake.

Gus is more discerning because, like me, he truly cares about the ingredients and how they are handled. "Tell me why you are excited about this cupcake."

It's an insightful question, which doesn't surprise me one bit. Gus wants to know the "why" more than the "what".

I point to the frosting. "Normally, a red velvet cupcake has a cream cheese frosting. It pairs nicely and is what people expect. Cuts the sweetness, especially when the baker remembers to add enough lemon to the cream cheese to amplify the necessary tartness component. But that didn't thrill me. It didn't make me want to put it on my website. In fact, when I contemplated making it my flavor of the month, I was embarrassed that I would do something that didn't sing to me. That's not what my bakery is about."

Gus' hand over his heart is my favorite thing. It's as if my passion for cupcakes is the moving aria of an opera he has been waiting his whole life to witness. "Tell me more."

I slide the cupcakes to them with trepidation and a

sliver of surety. This cupcake is a winner. Even if the world doesn't love or accept it, I know it is a stellar creation.

"This one, I am proud to have on my menu. It's a red velvet cupcake, but instead of the standard cream cheese frosting, I've done a lemon ricotta cream cheese filling, with a raspberry buttercream. It doesn't have the overly sweet notes, nor is it the fluffy frosting you would find on a grocery store cupcake. Ricotta has bones to it to balance out the sweetness of the frosting. It has depth that doesn't want to be whipped without thought. But the flavors marry well with the sweet cake. Plus, I tamed the sweetness of the cake with black pepper. Now there is a balance that takes something that normally wouldn't belong on a cupcake, and makes it sing."

Hunter grimaces. "Black pepper in a cupcake?"

I beam at him. "Of course!"

Gus doesn't question my recipe. "Balance is important. That was my focus with the clam chowder. See how the flavors married nicely?"

My neck shrinks. "I've actually never tried the soup. Clams look weird."

Hunter tilts his head at me as if I have said something shocking, which I guess I have, given that I've been cooking here and have yet to try the soups I've been making.

Gus merely laughs at my confession. "That's a crime we can solve right now." Gus gets up from the table and disappears into the kitchen. He returns with a cup of the steaming soup and three spoons. He hands one to Hunter as he resumes his spot in the booth across from me, sliding the cup toward me. "I try your cupcake, and you try my soup."

I gather my gumption and blow on the broth, readying myself for the feat I have chickened out on every day I've come into this place.

The first bite doesn't have a clam on it, thank goodness.

My eyes close as the flavors dance on my tongue. It's not a heavy tomato flavor. The broth makes room for the carrots, onions, and the bay leaf, so they all sing together. It's light without being watery, flavorful without being a mess of salt in your mouth.

"Cheater," Hunter hisses, pressing the ice to his cheek. "You didn't get a clam that time."

I narrow an eye at him and then go for the gold. It takes a fair bit of bravery to scoop a clam onto my spoon and shove the thing into my mouth.

Hunter laughs at me. "You can't make that face before you've even tasted it!"

"Oh, yes I can," I say around the mouthful. But when I finally bite into the thing, it's not the slimy slug I was envisioning. It's not chewy like a gummy bear, but delicate and soft. When I bite down, tomato flavor explodes through my mouth, granting me the powerful note of acid to balance the broth perfectly.

I stare down at the cup in wonder. "Oh, Gus. This is incredible!"

Gus covers his mouth through a laugh. "You made it."

"It's your recipe. Oh, wow. I can see why people come back for bowl after bowl of this stuff."

Hunter and Gus take their spoons, readying for their turn on the taste-test schedule.

Gus does his due diligence, poking at the cupcake beneath to test the crumb. He samples the cake and the icing separately to get a handle on both flavors. He lets it sit on his tongue and remain in his mouth for longer than a few seconds, so he can examine the different notes of the dessert's separate parts. "Oh, that black pepper. You didn't hold back. I might turn into a sweets person if more desserts tasted like this."

Then he tries a bite of both the sections together, as the cupcake was meant to be sampled.

His eyes close. There is an intake of breath, followed by a contented exhale. Then a low "mm" sound that revives any hardened parts of my soul.

Watching someone take their first bite of my cupcake is the most satisfying thing in the world. More than watching a flower bloom. More than the beauty of a freshly fallen snow. When someone loves my cupcake and lets the flavors change the trajectory of their day, it is a privilege I will never tire of watching.

Hunter munches his cupcake like a barbarian, getting frosting on his nose and smearing the red crumbs on his chin. "Whoa," he comments, his mouth full of fresh-baked joy. "This cupcake is huge!"

Then the experience takes him over, as well. It's the best day ever, because I get to watch one swoon of satisfaction, followed by a second.

Hunter slams his palm on the table and then scrunches his fingers near the side of his mouth, giving an enthusiastic chef's kiss to christen the dessert as his new favorite thing. "Incredible!" he marvels.

I lean back in the booth, counting the day as a win. Maybe the universe is throwing me a bone, giving me two of my happiest moments right in a row to make up for the fact that I nearly died not half an hour ago.

But as Gus goes in for another bite, waxing poetic about the ricotta cheese filling, and how he would love to spread it on a toasted, buttered baguette, I know that the world isn't done with me yet.

I have more cupcakes to bake, more friends to make, and more of life to learn about as I wake up every morning in this cozy town of Sweetwater Falls.

21

AUNT WINNIE IN A RED DRESS

*A*unt Winnie has had her red dress on since early this morning, even though the Live Forever Club's Valentine's Day party isn't until the afternoon.

Logan, Carlos, Marianne and I have been working nonstop to get the Soup Alleyoop transformed into a Roaring Twenties-themed atmosphere for the party that everyone has been talking about.

There are two shifts, because there were so many RSVPs. The younger crowd's party starts at five o'clock, while the seniors get their own slot and first pick of the refreshments because their party starts at two o'clock.

Leave it to my aunt and her two wacky friends to throw two parties in one day, and whine that they didn't think to throw a third for the younger children.

"It's perfect. I mean absolutely beautiful," I remark to Marianne. "You really outdid yourself."

Marianne crosses her arms over her chest, surveying her handiwork. While the Live Forever Club chose the theme and gave their input on the decorations, it was Marianne who truly brought it all to life.

I came with a stapler and tape, and stuck things where Marianne directed all over Gus' restaurant, which has been completely transformed.

Everything is lavish, including the dark red tapestries hanging from floor to ceiling in the four corners of the dining area. The basketball hoops have been either cranked up toward the ceiling or covered by the red draperies.

Each booth has a theme, which gives the place an extra quirk to keep us in the game of pretending we are living in a different era.

I straighten out my flapper dress, which has fringe from shoulder to waist, and then more pink glittering fringe from waist to knee. I am a shimmering pink disco ball, with my hair in a pretty knot that Aunt Winnie fashioned to the left side of my head this morning.

My lipstick is red, which isn't normally a color I would gravitate toward. But as afternoon turns to evening, I am loving this step outside my comfort zone.

In fact, this dress is a full leap outside my comfort zone, and I'm cherishing every swish of my hips, because this gown is fabulous.

Marianne shakes her hips for no reason other than to

see her green-hued flapper dress swish back and forth. "We should wear these every day. My normal clothes are going to feel so boring tomorrow."

I cross my arms over my chest. "That settles it. On Sunday, we're wearing these dresses again while we go about our normal days. They deserve to be worn, and worn often."

Marianne grins at the scandal of wearing something so lavish without the excuse of the occasion. "Deal."

Carlos makes himself useful serving desserts to the guests, dressed as an old timey bartender. Marianne motions to the woman operating the drink cart. Her normally meek demeanor is eclipsed by her outfit, which doesn't hold back. She commands the room with ease, which is a sight I wish I could see on the daily. Marianne isn't the librarian right now. She is Marianne the Wild, laughing at jokes and offering beverages to the senior citizens who make this town the colorful place it is.

I love it here. When Hunter comes in the door with a gentleman date on his arm, I know it's just about time for the older crowd to shuffle out and the younger group to make themselves at home for a Valentine's Day extravaganza.

But a beautiful thing happens that I did not expect. As more and more people around my generation come into the Soup Alleyoop, they don't seek out chairs, but start dancing in the center of the restaurant. But they don't all dance with the people they came in with; they mingle with the older crowd and bring them out to join in the dancing.

My grin cannot be stopped when I see guys around my age asking the older women to dance who must have babysat them back when they were little. The women light up as if they are being told they are the prettiest belles of the ball, and they join their new partners on the dance floor with glee and scandal all over their lovely faces. The women my age are doing the same, asking the older men for a spin on the dance floor.

I don't know why the sight brings moisture to my eyes. Perhaps my heart is full because it is a heady thing to be surrounded by happiness and love.

Joy bubbles out from every corner, lifting each spirit because we did not come here for the exclusive goal of checking a romantic box and calling it a day. We came here because we love our lives in this sweet small town. This sort of celebration might not happen anywhere else in the world, which means that of all the places we could be spending our holiday, there is no place else that we would rather be.

When Logan sidles up to me at the punch bowl after he finishes replenishing the appetizers, he kisses my temple. Then he turns to Aunt Winnie, who is happily clapping to the music beside me. "You're too pretty to be standing on the sidelines tonight, Winifred. Feel like teaching me a thing or two? I have a feeling I'm going to make a complete fool of myself if I ask your niece for a dance first. I need you to show me how to impress her."

Aunt Winnie beams at Logan and takes his hand without hesitation. "I'd be glad to show you a few moves, Logan. Can't have you stepping all over Charlotte's toes, can we."

Logan and my great-aunt grin at each other while she does, in fact, do her best to teach him how to up his game.

My hand goes over my mouth when I see the work she has cut out for her. To say that Logan has two left feet is an understatement.

Karen moves to my side, giggling at the sight. "Oh, my. Winnie didn't know what she was getting herself into, taking Logan for a spin." She pats my hand with her bony fingers. "Don't worry, Charlotte. We'll set his feet straight for you."

When Logan steps on Aunt Winnie's toe and can't stop apologizing, I laugh louder than I mean to.

I turn to Karen, elated at how the night is unfolding. "Feel like a dance?"

Karen beams at me, her wiry smile lighting up her entire being. "If you think you can keep up. I've gotta warn you, if you're as bad a dancer as your boyfriend, I might ditch you in the middle of the dance floor."

"I consider myself warned."

Karen and I join the dancers, reminding me that it's been a hot minute since I've done any sort of dancing that required rhythm or finesse. I do my best to keep up with Karen, who never waits for anyone, but determines her own steps in life.

It does my heart good when the center of the scrum hollows out because Gus and Agnes are tearing it up in ways that people my age can't come close to keeping up with. Their hands move in perfect synchronization. Their feet fly with exuberance that denies the ages on their birth certificates.

Pretty soon, we are all clapping in time for the precious couple who waited years to give themselves permission to dance together in public.

Dwight joins them in the center, dressed as a giant heart-shaped box of chocolates. He pirouettes around them in one of his many enormous mascot costumes, adding to the oddity and joy of the day.

Because of course Dwight has a costume for Valentine's Day.

Only here. Only in Sweetwater Falls would a party like this go down and a celebration like this last well into the night. As the hours tick by, the dancing never comes to a complete stop.

By the end of the party, my feet are sore, but my heart is filled with gratitude for the place that took me in and turned me from a girl with a dream into Charlotte the Brave.

The End.

Love the book?
Leave a review.

RED VELVET CUPCAKE RECIPE

Yield: 12 Jumbo Cupcakes or 18 Regular-Sized Cupcakes

From the cozy mystery novel *Red Velvet Villainy*
by Molly Maple

"It's a red velvet cupcake, but instead of the standard cream cheese frosting, I've done a lemon ricotta cream cheese filling, with a raspberry buttercream. It doesn't have the overly sweet notes, nor is it the fluffy frosting you would find on a grocery store cupcake. Ricotta has bones to it to balance out the sweetness of the frosting. It has depth that doesn't want to be whipped without thought. But the flavors marry well with the sweet cake. Plus, I tamed the sweetness of the cake with black pepper. Now there is a balance that takes something that normally wouldn't belong on a cupcake, and makes it sing."

-from Red Velvet Villainy

Ingredients for the Cupcake:

2½ cups all-purpose flour

1½ cups granulated sugar

2 tsp unsweetened cocoa powder

1 tsp salt

1 tsp baking soda

1½ cup vegetable oil

1 cup room temperature buttermilk

1 tsp vinegar

2 large eggs, room temperature

2 tsp red food coloring

1 tsp pure vanilla extract

Instructions for the Cupcake:

1. Preheat the oven to 350°F and line a cupcake pan with cupcake liners.

2. In a medium bowl, sift together 2½ cups flour, 1 tsp baking soda, 2 tsp baking cocoa and 1 tsp salt. Set flour mixture aside.

3. In a large bowl, use a mixer to beat the vegetable oil and sugar on medium speed for three minutes. Beat until shiny, scraping down the sides of the bowl as needed.

4. Add eggs one at a time while the mixer runs on low speed. Add 1 tsp pure vanilla extract

and 2 tsp red food coloring. Mix until
   smooth.

5. Stir 1 tsp vinegar into 1 cup buttermilk.

6. With the mixer on low speed, add the flour
   mixture in thirds, alternating with the
   buttermilk mixture. Mix to incorporate with
   each addition, scraping down the sides of the
   bowl as needed. Beat until just combined.

7. Divide the batter into your lined cupcake pan,
   filling each one 2/3 the way full.

8. Bake for 17-20 minutes at 350°F, or until a
   toothpick stuck in the center comes out clean.

9. Let them cool in the pan for 10 minutes, then
   transfer to a cooling rack. Cool to room
   temperature before frosting.

Ingredients for the Filling:

½ cup ricotta cheese

½ cup cream cheese

½ tsp lemon zest

Instructions for the Filling:

1. Using a strainer or cheesecloth, strain your
   ricotta cheese for at least two hours, making
   sure to remove all excess moisture. (Best if
   strained overnight)

2. In your stand mixer, whip ½ cup ricotta cheese,

½ cup cream cheese and ½ tsp lemon zest until well combined. Set aside until cupcakes are done baking.

Ingredients for the Frosting:
2 sticks unsalted butter, softened
4 cups powdered sugar
2 tsp vanilla extract
1/3 cup raspberries

Instructions for the Frosting:

1. Place 2 sticks unsalted butter into stand mixer and beat until well combined.
2. Slowly add powdered sugar one cup at a time, alternating with vanilla extract until combined but not overmixed.
3. Mix in 1/3 cup raspberries. Beat until fluffy.

To Assemble the Cupcake:

1. Once cupcakes are cooked and cooled, put the ricotta cream cheese filling into a piping bag and insert into the center of each cupcake, squeezing in a generous amount.
2. Pipe the raspberry buttercream frosting on top.

FREE PREVIEW

Enjoy a free preview of *Buttercream Bloodshed*,
Book Eight in the Cupcake Crimes series:

22

BUTTERCREAM BLOODSHED PREVIEW

Knock Your Soup-Off

*O*f all the town events I never expected might rouse my competitive nature, the Knock Your Soup-Off event had me staying up late last night to prepare for what I am hoping will turn out to be a first-place entry.

My great-aunt Winnie sidles into the kitchen, her shoulder-length silver hair pulled away from her face in a bun. Her sea-green eyes sparkle with amusement that is mingled with pity. "Did you stay up late and get up early? Bad combination, honey cake."

I let out a laborious sigh of frustration at no one besides myself. "Yes. I swear, if I lose to Bill's broccoli cheese slop, I'm moving."

Aunt Winnie chortles, kissing my cheek on her way to the coffee pot. "The plus side is that you made coffee already this morning. One less thing for me to do. The downside is that you actually might throttle Bill if he places ahead of you." Her mouth pulls to the side while she pours the black coffee into her teacup. "I'll have to remember to have my camera ready in case you do something like that. I'll want to remember baby's first violent crime."

I take a break from rolling mini meatballs so I can sip my coffee, which contains about a quarter cup of raspberry buttercream frosting to make the strong drink palatable. "I don't expect I'll win the golden soup pot, but I at least want to place ahead of Bill. That's the goal."

Aunt Winnie shakes her head. "Spoken like an underachiever, which you are not." She balls up her fist and raises it. "Go for the gold, Charlotte McKay. I plan on one of my girls winning this thing, because I want to eat out of a golden soup pot this year. Agnes is making her tomato soup with canned tomatoes from her garden. Karen is making broccoli cheese soup just to spite Bill. I'm making my specialty, which I have full confidence is a hit, and Marianne and Carlos are making chicken tortilla soup." She peers into my pot. "How many batches of this same recipe, slightly tweaked, have you made in the past two weeks?"

I stick the tray of mini meatballs into the oven and then tuck a stray blonde wave behind my ear. "My Italian wedding soup is going to be the best Italian wedding soup in the world. Not just the fair, but the world. Either that, or I've made this recipe so many times, I've gone insane, and the world is one giant meatball."

Aunt Winnie inhales deeply over the pot. "It smells like a warm blanket and a hug. It's a winner, Charlotte. I love watching you go all out for town events. It's like you were born to live here."

I chuckle at her phrasing. "I haven't even lived in Sweetwater Falls for a whole year yet. I never thought I would care this much about a soup contest, but I want that golden pot, Aunt Winnie."

"Then give it all you've got, Charlotte the Brave. Don't hold back."

I take her advice to heart and add in a touch more garlic into the next batch of meatballs.

And by "a touch more," I mean about a whole bulb extra.

Garlic is fuel for the soul.

I keep my nose in my soup for the next few hours, ignoring the sunrise, breakfast, and the bustling of the day around the house. In fact, I don't stop until Aunt Winnie shoos me upstairs to take a shower so we can get going.

When I come down, freshly showered (and hopefully not looking like I stayed up working on soup for an embarrassing number of hours), I feel like I am ready for this competition.

I load up the largest size slow cooker in existence,

then I mosey through the kitchen in search of Aunt Winnie's offering. "I can't find your pot of soup in the fridge, Aunt Winnie. Where is it? I can put it in the car for you."

Come to think of it, I've been so engrossed in my own soup that it only just now dawns on me that I haven't seen my great-aunt cooking at all. "You're entering the contest, right?"

Aunt Winnie smirks at me as she fits her arms through the sleeves of her light-green cardigan. "Mine's been done and ready. It's in a box by the front door. Mind helping me load it into the trunk?"

I tilt my head to the side. "When did you make your soup? I've been hogging the kitchen this week and didn't see you making yours."

Aunt Winnie flashes me a look filled with mischief. "Trust me, no one will complain about my soup. It'll be a huge hit. I'll assemble it once we get there."

My pitch climbs with nerves that a good night of sleep might have ironed out. "But the flavors have to sit overnight to marry well!" I pull from my recently-acquired knowledge gained from working at the Soup Alleyoop—a basketball-themed soup restaurant.

Aunt Winnie pats my hand. "I've got the recipe perfected."

I guess being ninety-one years old gives a person a certain credibility you don't have to stay up late to earn.

I drive slower than the thirty-five miles per hour speed

limit into town proper to make sure my slow cooker and Aunt Winnie's box of ingredients don't tip.

The small town of Sweetwater Falls pulls out all the stops when it comes to putting on events. There's always something going on around here, and today does not disappoint.

There is an enormous soup pot that doubles as a bubble blower to entertain the children. Though the March air is nippy, it only serves to send the bubbles flying far and wide. Big and small, the bubbles are everywhere, landing on surfaces and popping on people's clothes. It's an added element of magic I didn't realize the world needed.

Dwight is wearing a mascot costume of a giant soup cracker—a costume I didn't realize existed or would ever be put to use. He waves proudly at the kids, welcoming guests and directing them to the table where they can grab up a steaming beverage, along with a ballot to select their personal favorite soup.

It costs ten dollars for a taste of every pot of soup at the fair, which is a bargain no one hesitates to pay. Rip, the Town Selectman, is wearing a hat with a felt soup bowl atop his salt-and-pepper hair, his megaphone pressed to his lips. "Come one, come all! The Knock Your Soup-Off is about to start. All soups must be at your station and ready to serve in one minute!" Then to the line of people congregating around the ticket exchange, he gives a blustery, "Put your donations in the soup pot and grab a ballot. Remember, all proceeds from the event go toward restoring the foot bridges down by the falls." He clutches the fabric over his heart, a wistful look on his features. "Think of how beautiful the falls will be with several footbridges in place to take you closer to nature's best. And if that doesn't turn your crank, then think of the boost in tourism! That's right. All the soup you can eat, plus a thriving economy."

There's a Maypole with colorful ribbons streaming down in the center of the fair. The long tables of entrants are in a U-shape around the perimeter of the town square, sheltered from the sun by red awnings.

I position my pot and then Aunt Winnie's box of ingredients on our designated spots, grateful to see that we're all stationed near each other.

It wouldn't be a proper town event without Agnes, Karen, Marianne, Carlos, and Logan.

Everyone else is already set up, so they help Aunt Winnie and me get situated, plugging in my pot into the power strip and opening Aunt Winnie's box for her.

Karen's barking laughter takes me by surprise. "Oh, Winnie. If I've never told you I love you, this tips it. I love you. Never leave my side." She cups her bony hands around her mouth. "Everyone, the contest is over! We have the winner right here!"

Curious as to what could possibly be in the box, I lean over Karen's slender shoulder to take a peek.

My laughter comes out a snort as I tuck my blonde

curls back and resituate my purple knitted hat that Agnes made me. "That's not your soup, is it?"

Aunt Winnie sets out her pot and starts opening bottles of whiskey, pouring them inside with no hint of another ingredient anywhere in sight. "I told you; everyone's going to love my soup. Whiskey neat. Can't go wrong."

Carlos laughs and points to her pot. "I'll be stopping by to sample your soup first, Winnie."

Logan greets me with a hug once my slow cooker is plugged in and the stack of cups are set up beside my pot. "I brought your good luck charms." He points to my goldfish bowl, where Buttercream is flicking her tail at the change of scenery. "Stopped by the Bravery Bakery this morning before coming here. I knew you'd want Buttercream to be here for this. She's always good luck for you."

While I'm not a huge fan of public displays, I can't help but kiss Logan's shaved cheek. He smells like soap, aftershave, and kindness, which is a heady combination. "Thank you. And I see you brought Baby Bill."

Logan tucks the eight-inch knitted doll of one of my favorite residents of Sweetwater Falls into my arms once I release him. "Of course. I thought if the real Bill doesn't want to taste your soup and admit defeat, the doll of him could at least pretend. You could even make him cry. Or worse, you could make him be nice to people. The possibilities are endless."

I smile up at Logan, grateful that he gets me, and that

he goes the extra few miles just to make me smile. "Thank you. Plus, the real Bill hates it when I carry this thing around. Bonus."

Logan touches my nose just to be cute. "Why do you think I *really* brought it? He was a jerk to my dad yesterday. Getting under Bill's skin is going to be my new hobby today."

I cuddle my Doll Bill to my chest, loving that the likeness of him looks just as surly as the real thing.

The wind changes direction, blowing a savory heaven straight into my nose. "Oh, that's amazing. I can't wait to try everyone's soups." I fidget with my ladle, making sure it's positioned near my pot for easy access. "I always think of soup for the fall months, but we're heading into spring."

Marianne's head bobs, her chocolate-colored short haircut swishing across her cheeks. "Oh, this event used to be held in the fall, but people ate more soup than the cooks could keep up with, so we switched it to the spring, where people don't feel the need to guzzle a pot of soup in one sitting."

Carlos chuckles at the logic. "I love it." He points his finger at the row of soups that stretches to include several dozen varieties. "I swear, if we lose to another chicken tortilla soup, I'm going to sample Winnie's whole pot."

Aunt Winnie reaches up and pinches Carlos' cheeks.

It doesn't take long for the fair to fill up. There are people I know and love, but so many more that I've never seen before.

"I don't recognize like, half of these people," I tell Carlos and Marianne as I ladle portion after portion, handing out the cups as people filter through the line with eager anticipation on their faces.

Carlos snorts. "Well, that's better than me. I recognize less than half."

Marianne smiles as she hands out her cups of soup from behind the long row of tables. "The soup fair is a big deal in Hamshire. Rip advertises it there to get the most amount of people to come into town. We'll see a big boost in business this week because of the extra foot traffic. Rip really wants those footbridges for the waterfalls."

"Ah. That makes more sense."

The ladles are all the same model, serving up exactly a third a cup of soup per customer. Every detail is perfectly organized and well thought through.

I wave to Ivan, who is paying for his entry ticket. He waves back, letting me know we'll catch up when he makes his way to my soup. I haven't seen Ivan face to face in months. I love that I've become so comfortable in my new hometown that I am inviting outside people to events as if I totally belong here.

Which, I guess I do.

I first met Ivan a few months ago when I went to run an errand for my friend Lisa, picking something up for her at the gym in Hamshire. Ivan and I got along well, even if one of the first few times we chatted, he admitted to losing his temper after an investment went south, which resulted in him roughing up the man who cheated him.

But whenever we interact, that's not the man I know. Ivan is a softspoken gentle giant, with a neck thicker than my thigh. He treats the gym as a sanctuary, which is the only time I have garnered an appreciation for lifting heavy things.

I am desperate to get out from behind my pot of soup and try the various offerings that are making my mouth water, but I stand dutifully by my pot and serve portion after portion for the next two hours.

I love how happy everyone sounds. The children are chasing bubbles while the adults are rubbing their bellies contentedly.

But when a scream ripples out across the town square twenty minutes later, every head turns toward the source of the sound.

I squint to see if I can make out the shape of the person who looks like they've fainted on the grass. Before I can stop myself, I am ducking under the table and running out to the felled man.

"Ivan?" I call out, horrified at the sight of the body-builder on the ground, his hand cupping his throat as yellow foam spills from his lips.

Logan is by my side, already on his phone, calling the paramedics. "Did anyone see what happened?" he calls out, kneeling beside the man I invited to this event, which apparently is giving him some sort of horrible reaction.

We've texted a few times. Ivan asks me if I plan on making working out a regular thing (no), and I ask him if he's taken any sunlit walks in the great outdoors (also no).

I invited him to this event, hoping he would have something outside of the gym to add to his bodybuilding schedule.

Frank points to the cup of chili that's spilled out onto the grass beside Ivan's straining body. "He had a bite of the chief's chili, keeled over and collapsed! Someone do something!"

I hold Ivan's hand as his eyes close. I haven't seen Ivan in months. Our interactions were friendly and far too few. I should have visited him and forced him to go out for more walks so he could enjoy the sunshine outside of the gym where he spent so many mornings. I should have come by any time in the past several months, but I didn't, counting this event as a good amount of time invested in a friendship.

I should know how to do more than simply hold his hand while his eyes close and his pulse fades beneath my fingertips. "Ivan," I whisper over and over again.

The sheriff stands in horror behind his pot of chili, frozen in shock that something he made might be suspect in harming another person. He stares at Ivan with wide eyes, saying nothing as his mouth freezes in a shocked "O" shape.

Logan does chest compressions after checking that nothing was lodged in Ivan's throat.

But Ivan doesn't stir. Without Logan's help of pumping over and over in hopes of getting him to breathe on his own, Ivan's body would be motionless.

"No," I whisper, horrified that I invited a man to an event at which he might be taking his last breath. "Ivan, no!"

By the time the ambulance gets to the fair, Ivan's pulse cannot be found. I hear pitters and patters of gossip that fan out around us. The last meal Ivan had was a sample of Sheriff Flowers' chili.

Author Molly Maple believes in the magic of hot tea and the romance of rainy days.

She is a fan of all desserts, but cupcakes have a special place in her heart. Molly spends her days searching for fresh air, and her evenings reading in front of a fireplace.

Molly Maple is a pen name for USA Today bestselling fantasy author Mary E. Twomey, and contemporary romance author Tuesday Embers.

Visit her online at www.MollyMapleMysteries.com. Sign up for her newsletter to be alerted when her next new release is coming.

Made in the USA
Middletown, DE
28 March 2022

63274227R00120